Some great stories. Loved it

INCIDENTS INVOLVING WARMTH
🔲🔲🔲🔲🔲🔲🔲🔲🔲🔲🔲🔲🔲🔲🔲🔲🔲🔲🔲🔲🔲🔲🔲
by Anna Livia

radical feminist and lesbian publishers

Published by Onlywomen Press, radical feminist and lesbian publishers, 38 Mount Pleasant, London WC1X 0AP, UK.

Cover design Tyra Till
Photo by Fiona Graph
Typesetting: Columns, Reading, Berkshire.

Bedrock Passion was first published in SPINSTER No. 5
Mind The Gap was first published in EVERYDAY MATTERS TWO, Sheba Feminist Publishers, 1984.
1 Woman = 7 Cups of Tea was first published in THE REACH and Other Stories, edited by Lilian Mohin & Sheila Shulman, Onlywomen Press, 1984.
5½ Charlotte Mews is to be published in STEPPING OUT, edited by Ann Oosthuizen, published by Pandora Press.

Printed and bound in Great Britain by Redwood Burn Ltd., Trowbridge, Wiltshire.

Cover printed by Duxford Press, London EC1

British Library Cataloguing in Publication Data
Livia, Anna
    Incidents Involving Warmth
    I. Title
    823′. 914[F]   PR6062
    ISBN 0-906500-21-4

for Lilian Mohin

Acknowledgements:
I would like to take this opportunity to thank Anna Wilson,
Ellen Galford, Ellen Smyth, Fiona Graph, RaeAnn
Robertson & Susan Morse for helping me move flat [Lilian
was sick that day]. Also Jacky Bishop, who had to go to
work. And finally, Dympna Jones, my mother, for her
sudden concentration and rare brilliance.

Born Dublin 1955. Scorpio ram. Oh alright then, sheep.
Childhood in Africa; adolescence ın London; mother in
Australia. Lesbian radical feminist. Still no sign of a pension
plan, health ınsurance or a mortgage. Would settle for a
secure tenancy.

Published work:
  RELATIVELY NORMA [Onlywomen Press 1982]
  a novel
  ACCOMMODATION OFFERED [Women's Press 1985]
  a   nother novel

CONTENTS

FAY KING MEETS RAE CONGER

Fay had tried knocking and banging; she had tried shoes, hammers, fists, the garlic crusher, the electric drill; she had tried shouting and yelling, knocking on his door and leaving notes. She had tried slamming her own door eight times in succession. She had tried going out and ringing herself up from the call box, placing her receiver right next to the dividing wall. To no avail: the call stopped after ten minutes and thirty seconds. She had tried turning her radio up full blast as soon as he started, but he seemed to like it. She experimented with different stations. Radio One was out, obviously. Opera wasn't bad, and the BBC World Service was really rather good, with its utterly arbitrary stress on entirely inappropriate words: "From Tuesday *12th* March *All* 9½ pence stamps will be with*drawn*". When she stumbled onto the Stock Market in German, she thought her prayers had been answered. But if her next-door-neighbour were a refugee who had survived the last war, a German broadcast would be a far graver and more terrifying experience than was merited by the continuous playing of hollow wallow.

One evening, as Fay tuned to whatever station it is that specialises in the 'The Wombles of Wimbledon Common', she heard, not the reducing of volume next door, but an answering blast from downstairs and 'The Hallelujah Chorus' rent the air. The far end of the corridor replied with 'Send In The Clowns'. Soon the whole estate was competing in a cacophony only the cops could stop. Whilst 'Je Ne Regrette Rien' would have walked off with quite a few prizes, still it was the 'Hallelujah' which really raised the roof. Fay's neighbour switched unperturbed from 'Eleanor Rigby' to 'Land of Hope and Glory'.

Though she had yet to meet him, Fay knew her neighbour

like the seven year itch. At five to nine, after his morning gargle with 'No More Lonely Nights', he set off for work. Pink collar obviously. Home by five forty-five and a quick shot of 'Sounds of Silence'. Bath. Dinner. Liver and bacon usually. Round nine he went down the pub. Back at eleven and 'A Nightingale Sang in Berkeley Square' or 'Do You Wanna Be In my Gang?'. Depending. A triumphal blast of 'Surf's Up' about three a.m. if he was celebrating. Fortunately, his affairs were mostly casual. His divorce was recent as his kids still got dumped on him at the weekend, adding 'Mucho Macho Duck' to his repertoire.

The battle was, in the end, not so much conceded, as superceded. Fay's short-life would be up. She would move, as she had had to move every six months of her lesbian past. Not for her the outraged tenant: "You can't get me out. I bin ere twenty years." Nor even the successful but nostalgic: "Two and a half years I stayed in that dump." Fay never knew whether to buy a shopping trolley, bath plugs that fitted or a real bed. Would it be furnished? Far from the shops? She wound a jay cloth round the plug from her last move but one and decided to get some white gloss. You always needed that. She weighed up options: there was sharing, which involved either paying the other woman's phone bill, or hours of sympathetic listening, compensation for not splitting her wine bill. There was squatting still, but to improvise stand pipes and plasterboard ceilings you had to be at least four people which quadrupled the phone bill and the listening. There was private rented with its 'first to the front door with five hundred in cash', plus months of fair-renting and associated bitterness. Fay was so involved in the contemplated horrors of the chase that she barely noticed when her neighbour swapped 'Return To Sender' for 'Knock Three Times on the Ceiling if You Want Me'.

Over the next week, Fay wrote applications to every housing association she'd ever heard of, including hostels for single men. She took a day off work to ring round, following up the letters. She provoked fellow co-op members into meeting. They asked the Trust who'd provided short life if there'd be any more, or even, though they hesitated over the word, something permanent. The Trust explained, patiently, that it was in the nature of the short not to be long. Or some such. Fay brought the letter to the next meeting: their vicious circle on headed notepaper.

As 'Walking Back to Happiness' followed 'The First Time Ever I Saw Your Face', Vicky turned to Fay,

"Which one is he, then?"

"You know, I don't think I've ever seen him. I've banged on his door, don't know how many times, but he's never answered."

"It's the woofter, isn't it, Ro? Pink collar, smells of onions."

"O O Only the Lonely. . ."

"Jesus, this is too bloody much. Would you turn the blasting volume down?" Marita yelled.

"I Talk To the Trees. . ."

"Tell him you'll call the cops," Vicky advised.

"No," yelped Rowan, "all I need's a bust, with what I'm carrying."

"Tell him you hope he dies of AIDS," said Marita.

"Don't remind him, or he'll send us a blood sample."

"Shut up, you two. Don't be wicked."

"Imbecilic. We may be the lowest risk group, but we're there."

"Papers say we are all the same anyway. Ambulance drivers put on their rubber gloves and shoot off as soon as look at us."

"Item Two on the Agenda, okay? Now back to Item One."

"If he won't answer, stick a note through his door saying we're trying to have a meeting and can't hear ourselves think."

"Oh yeah, he'll listen to reason."

Fay scribbled the message on a scrap of paper and stomped out. She knocked. Waited. Then pushed the note through the letter box. Shortly after came the long-forgotten, almost unbelievable sound of a stereo being turned down. Fay stared at the closed door in amazement. She was about to pad back to her own flat when she heard a little scraping noise, as of a letter box opened from inside. A note appeared. She pulled it free. Unfolded it.

"Come in," it said.

The clank of a door chain, of bolts drawn top and bottom,

of Ingersoll and Banham, rang out eerily in the now silent evening. The light in the passage went on; Fay found herself on the Welcome mat.

"Hello," said her neighbour, "I'm Rae Conger."

"Fay King," muttered Fay, "pleased to meet you."

Rae showed her into the sitting room; predictably, lined with l.p.s as others are with egg boxes. Fay sat on a comfortable old armchair, next to the muted ghetto blaster and between two speakers. The flat was otherwise a left-handed version of her own.

"Short for Marini," Rae explained easily, as though her name were the most surprising thing about her.

"Oh," gasped Fay. It was a relief to gasp.

"Well, dear," Rae continued, "I've been meaning to have a word with you. You see . . ."

Fay saw. Marini was gorgeous. Well-muscled and power-ful, with grey wings in her hair and chiselled lines across her face so that, as she talked, her eyebrows told the story too. Peaks and troughs laced them like the bedchart of danger. Deep ravines circled her mouth, and her left cheek was streaked by a sudden diagonal, running from nostril to jaw. Wiry and elastic, she would leave various limbs poised on the arm of a chair or a table, just long enough for the welling of admiration.

"I've come into some luck," said Rae, "I thought you might like a streak. Let me explain."

Fay let her.

"I, too, am a shortlifer. Probably for the same reason as you? Yes, I thought I detected a heightened sensitivity to the ways of women. Apart from some cassettes, tapes, records and videos – the basic necessities – all my possessions remain in cardboard boxes to facilitate the next move. I have now, by a peculiar chain of circumstances, which I am about to describe, come into a house, which I propose we share. We have been living together, as it were, for the best part of six months, and we seem to get along pretty well. You know my habits as I know yours. I play my record player rather too loud; you don't like to answer the phone. I nine to five it at the office, and you, I assume, are a German student. I know the hours you keep, the names of your friends, your love of opera. [Might I suggest that oiling the door would be easier on the hinges than slamming?]

Fay opened her mouth to protest.

"Oh please hear me out."

A plea from such a creature. A great poet borrowing your pen.

"I was on my way to work one morning, wondering would I end up living in the back of a VW in the suburbs. In the crush to get out at Chancery Lane someone bumped into me and grabbed my breast. A man smirked into his cashmere, but he was out the doors before I could shout. I passed him on the escalator. "More fun tomorrow," he whispered. "Oh fuck you, fuck you. Pinch my breast like a mint leaf by the wayside." Bloody lucky, as it turned out, that I didn't yell aloud. I would kill him, though, I knew that. If ever I got the chance.

As I walked up Gray's Inn, I noticed him behind me. I crossed to post a letter and let him overtake. By Verulam Street I'd nearly caught him up again. I thought I might turn off to Leather Lane for coffee. Though his silent control was worse than infuriating. In the corner of my eye I noticed a car coming out of Portpool Lane. It's such a short street, you don't expect any traffic in or out. Maybe I noticed the speed, the other traffic. I knew I must get off Gray's Inn.

I'd just reached the protection of a side building when I heard brakes screech and the first crash resounded, then a second and a third. On the corner was the car from Portpool, and someone crushed beneath. I ran forward. It was the man in cashmere.

"Help, help," I shouted, "an ambulance. Call the police."

The woman from Barbarella's came out and I took my coat off to put under the man's head. His body was caught under the front wheel but he was still alive and, strangely, conscious. I tried to free him. He was very bloody and a hideous colour. I pulled gently but it was plain that, unless I heaved, I would not get him clear. They always tell you not to move the victims of road accidents, but at times of stress it is easy to forget such things. I pulled again, and felt something stretch under my hands as though it was about to snap.

"Better not move him, love," advised the woman from Barbarella's. Only, unfortunately, I didn't hear. I wiped his face with my jumper and I whispered, "I'm going to break your back." Then I heaved till I could feel the stretching, then the snap.

"That's alright love," said the ambulance men, "we'll take over now."

"Oh thank God you're here," I cried brokenly, close to weeping. The Barbarella woman gave me a cup of tea while we waited for the cops.

"Back's broken, Reg."

"No hope?"

"No. He's gone."

I burst into tears and wrung my hands.

"My God, it's all my fault. I should never have tried to move him."

"Well we do advise members of the public that unless they know what they're doing. ."

"It's not your fault, love. She did her best, you know. Wiped his face with her own jumper."

I told the police exactly what I'd seen. They said I was an excellent witness. The man sustained heavy internal injuries. It was certainly not my fault. But they could not convince me. I was very upset.

I had to appear in court. Chief witness for the prosecution. The police officer took me aside: the man in cashmere's mother had been asking for me. Could I bear to speak to her? I nodded tearfully. She was a nice elderly woman in navy blue wool, said her son had disgraced the family.

"He hadn't the calibre of a bank robber; nothing but the most cowardly, degrading crimes for my boy. But he is still my boy. And in his cowardly, degraded life, my dear, you were the last to treat him with common decency and even kindness. I heard how you wiped his blood with your own jumper. He leaves no mourners but me, nothing to anyone but a house in West London he bought with his petty pilfering. As his sole survivor, I have signed over the deeds to you. It's a sad day when a mother must be heir to her son."

So, how would you like the top floor of my new Elgin Crescent home? I would, of course, allow you free access to the communal gardens."

Fay reeled, gazing at Rae's knuckles with added respect. A flat. She had just been offered a flat. Fay was not too

12

stupefied to grasp the essentials. But her co-operative spirit clung close. Who needed the place most? As a lesbian co-op, their housing histories were necessarily grim.

"Don't," said Rae, as though intercepting Fay's thoughts. "You can't parcel it out, divide it fairly. Luck isn't like that. This is your streak. If you don't take it, no one else can have it. I'm only offering it to you."

"But the noise," Fay protested at last, "I can't bear that rubbish you play."

"A familiar ache," replied Rae, "you could start saving egg boxes."

A GOOD CRACK, SOMETIMES

One: Holly

"On Friday I went to Heathrow with Ruth. We were late because we'd been in bed, and it was all such a rush: snatching a boarding pass, waving tickets, gabbling flight numbers, (she had to take her luggage through herself, way past the final call) that I didn't have time to say 'I'll miss you'. I felt terrible looking round the airport, other people's lost goodbyes, unshared memories that divided us: twenty years ago, my mother stuffing my sister's woolly suits in litter bins, because we were overweight and it would be hot in Africa; ten years ago, Ruth's son, still thinking her thoughts, going back to the States to live with his father. Difficult with that around us to remember that we two knew each other now, that Ruth was off to see this son get married. I wanted to phone him, tell him she wasn't ready to go yet, didn't know who she was leaving yet, get him to postpone the wedding till Ruth was more certain about me: she'd only had a month. (But already my life seemed changed out of recognition. How dare she just fade off like a glorious rainbow between two thunder claps?) I would describe the dress she'd bought (thick green silk it was, it made me blush to see her try it on) and her son would know that, if his mother bought a dress, it was because she really did want to come to his wedding. (A dress at all, certainly, but that dress, soft and plunging.)

Ruth turned to me, no time even to ask what I was thinking. I kissed her and she disappeared through the barrier, leaving me with vague imaginings: her son, her ex-husband, a lover into whose arms she would descend from the plane; and stronger memories of my own: my little cousin waving goodbye and asking 'Mummy, will they be home for tea-time?'; anxiously studying a photograph of my father to make sure I'd recognise him when we got off at Africa. Already Ruth had gone and already I was drifting off. That's why she asks me what I'm thinking, to make sure I'm thinking about her. And so often I'm not. And so often I am.

But then I had to go to work and we were so busy, what with the new counter, flinging quiches and fresh cream cakes on the shelves, cutting sandwiches into mad quarters, cling-filming the couscous, that we didn't turn the coffee tap off for the first two hours, just kept pouring, spilling and handing out. Not two minutes to rub together in that place. Occasionally, as I applied a blue catering plaster to Carmel's cut finger, or pressed for a glass of milk, waiting for its slow white trickle, the only thing in the place obstinately taking its time, I would remember Ruth's post card during a row: "Can we have afterwards now, please? Already, I miss you"; the time in bed when she asked what was the matter and I scrabbled for a pen, and even then I went to the toilet while she read it: "I wish you loved me. When I'm kissing you like this, I wish that's what we were doing. It makes me cry." As I cut delicately round the grapefruit segments and stuffed a cherry in the middle, I wondered what I could have said at the airport that we did not already know."

Two: Flora

"On Friday my old mother put the electric kettle in a sinkful of water. I'd specially bought her one that turns off by itself but she says the little red light would go on and get her all confused. She used to have a normal one with a whistle, that you put on the gas, but she scalded herself – she can't see very well, got a cataract in one eye – and anyway, she said she could taste the aluminium. She used to collect her pension from the post office, but I had to go in and ask them to pay her in fifty pence pieces, cos she used to throw the pound notes in the litter bin. She eats a lot of mint galaxy, you see, and she thought the notes were sweetie papers. I can understand it. Those notes feel very crisp when they're new. So I thought up the fifty pences, cos she needs them anyway for the meter, and, when she pays for things, she can work out how much gas she'd be using and then she knows if it's expensive. When I said about the fifty pences at the Post Office, they asked me was she a bit? A bit? I said, she's completely. But then she always was. Why doesn't she go to the Old Pals' Club? they said, get her meals dirt cheap there. Dirt? she said, when I told her, muck's more like. She may be 78, but she wasn't born in this country and she likes a decent cup of coffee. She makes it in a sock. That's French, that is. Fills the pot in the morning, leaves it on the stove and it does her for the rest of the day. Thinking about it, one of the new machines we've got at work'd suit her down to the ground. It's real filter coffee, plumbed so you don't have to bother about water; all you do is press the button for a cup. I could bring her the refills from work.

No, but it did worry me what they said. She hasn't always lived opposite me, used to be in a Home. I'd lost contact with her, my family's like that, so I didn't even know. Terrible place, sounded like. There was this woman there, been in a mental hospital since she was fourteen, unmarried mother, that was where they put them when she was young. Course, by the time she was 75 she was completely loony. Well you would be. Social worker said hospital wasn't the place for her and they moved her to the Home. Lot of them there like that, wrecked or wretched. Staff treated my mother alright cos she's always been able to stand up for herself, knows the rules you see. It was only 'sheltered', not residential like Sunny Pastures, meant you had to be mobile, but you got a room to yourself and a bit of privacy. My mother had taken a fall and put her back out. Had to use a wheelchair. Daren't ask to move to the ground floor, case they said she couldn't look after herself. She got by with the aid of two home helps and every week, to prove mobility, she would wheel herself along the corridor to the top of the steps, clamber down painfully with a stick and the banisters, then heave herself into another wheelchair waiting at the bottom, and go and visit the warden. But she said they were cruel to the little people and she couldn't bear that. They used to count out toilet paper, forget to unlock the mail box, had this joke about 'Old ladies eat Complan' so they could make off with legs of mutton. No really, it was common knowledge, case of everyone knew but no one said. So, just before Christmas, my mother sent out a lot of cards, thank you notes to various charities. No one thought anything of it, it being the season, but she got that place closed down. Big enquiry; it reached the papers. Well, no one wanted an old battle axe after that, even if she was the local heroine.

I don't like going out and leaving her, case one of these days she ups and offs. Not that she isn't a worry to me, I can't say that, but it was much worse when I didn't know was she alive or dead or was the next customer complaining the coffee was too weak going to turn out to be her. She makes me wonder who's going to look after me; will they lose patience if I linger over dying so I have to disguise a plea for help as season's greetings?

But I was going to be late for work, so I filled the big thermos for her and hoped it wouldn't give her ideas."

Three: Carmel

"On Friday, at one o'clock in the morning, my husband boarded up all the windows, told me and the kids to get down on the floor. He said the English were coming and we'd better lie low. There'd been a bomb in Saint Jameses, blasted a military march past. It was in all the papers and a reconstruction on the telly to jog people's memories, gave you a number to ring if you'd seen anything suspicious. Only eleven injured, no one dead, but three of the horses had to be put down and, as my husband says, if the Brits are to have pity for anything, it's got to bend its back and walk on all fours. Some of them felt so pitiful about those horses, when they heard it was the Provos did it, that they didn't bother ringing any number, just went out and stuffed burning rags through the local Irish shop.

I took the tube home from work that night, for some

18

reason my husband couldn't fetch me. I'd just reached the bottom of the escalator when a woman asked was it the right platform for Piccadilly. I told her yes, only she'd have to change at Oxford Circus, and these three blokes heard my accent.

'Fucking Paddy,' they taunted, 'fucking Irish murderer. You don't deserve British protection.'

'We should leave you Barbarians to kill each other.'

'All line up and we'll shoot you, do a better job.'

'Leave the poor girl alone,' said the woman who wanted Piccadilly, 'what's she got to do with it?'

'Her lot blew up a parade of bloody horses,' one replied, 'what had they done to anyone?'

'Had to be put down,' the other nodded, but they began to lumber off. The other one turned to me like he didn't want to let go yet.

'I wish my sister was here,' he said, 'I just wish my sister was here. She loves horses and she can't stand you bog Irish Paddies.'

When he said about his sister, I giggled. I'd been so scared, you know, and now he was threatening me with his sister. So he hit me. Only slapped me across the face, but he looked like he couldn't go away unless he hit me.

'No one laughs at my sister,' he said.

I wasn't going to tell my husband, because of how he reacts, but I had to miss the train those blokes got on, so I was late home. Even then I didn't say very much, probly made it worse cos his imagination's very fertile. He listened, asked did anyone intervene, then offered to make me some hot milk. I was glad he took it so normal, wasn't in one of his funny moods. He goes up and down you see. When he's down, he shakes his head and won't go to work. When he's up , he keeps rushing around deciding things. Excitable. This time, he got me a hot water bottle and said he'd come to bed presently. Next thing I know he's got me and the kids lying on the floor in our dressing gowns.

'It's alright,' he says, 'I've everything under control. When they come, they'll find me ready for them.'

He dragged the dining room table, the wardrobe, the kids' blackboard, odd bits of wood, anything he could lay hands on up against the windows. Then he got the hammer and was going to nail everything up. I was worried about the neighbours. He'd already made a lot of noise, and one o'clock in the bloody morning's a fine time to rearrange the furniture. But what were they going to think if he started crashing and hammering? Him, he was alright, by morning he'd have slept it off, see it as a wise precaution but no longer necessary and go round clawing all the nails out again. And what about the kids? Are they sposed to believe the English are out to get them or that their Dad's a raving lunatic?

Sometimes it's a relief to go to work just to get away from it all."

Four: Holly

"When the queue finally died down and filed into the showroom, me and Carmel got two orange crates and sat down behind the counter. As Carmel says: 'If they can't see your heads, sometimes it puts them off asking'. I fetched us both cups of tea – with milk from the machine, not those liquid chalk cartons we feed the customers – and wondered whether to tell Carmel about Ruth, but she got in first.

'Holly,' she said, taking the tea bag out of the cup, 'David reckons Jonathan's youknow, goes both ways.'

'No,' I said, 'just the one.'

'Oh,' said Carmel, 'but what about his wife? (Shrug). I spose she doesn't know.'

'Not much wives don't know.'

'True enough,' she said, 'But you'd never have guessed would you? I mean, David you can tell, but Jonathan? Why do some of them try to hide it?'

'Mmm,' I shrugged, 'don't want to get hit on the head?'

Silence.

'Carmel,' I said.

'Yes?' she said.

'You know I am,' I said.

'Oh,' she said, 'I thought you were. David said he thought you were, youknow, like that.'

20

'Oh I am,' I said, 'I'm just like that.'

'I'm fascinated by it,' said Carmel, 'so's my husband. He's fascinated too. About what they do n all. I mean, how did you? Were you always? Or did something happen?'

'Yes,' I said, 'something happened. I started doing what I wanted.'

'But weren't you, the first time? Your friend, wasn't it . . . embarrassing?'

'Terrifying.'

'What was it though? Did you just like her you know. Her body?'

'Ye e es,' I said, 'but I didn't know that yet. We'd been talking all evening and I'd never talked like that before.'

'No,' said Carmel slowly, 'men just don't understand, do they?'

'No,' I agreed, 'something else was happening you know. We weren't just talking. (Pause). I wanted to kiss her.'

'I know what you mean,' said Carmel. 'I have a friend. Years older than me. Old enough to be my mother. We hug each other n so on, oh just when she's going or you're upset or something; when I don't see her, it's just doing the washing and getting the kids up, but when she comes round you can end up with the cereal bowls still on the table and it's gone four o'clock! My husband, he says: 'Eye eye Carmel, you bit that way then?' But I tell him it's none of his business, which it isn't: men have no idea what goes on between women.'

Then Flora comes back from the toilet.

'What's none of whose business?' she asks, but the public come swarming out of the showroom, so me and Carmel set up a production line in coffees and lemon teas and Flora goes back on her till.

'Could I have it a bit weaker please, dear?'

'Where's the Parma ham? It says on the menu, 'Parma ham'.'

'What's in this? Jam?'

'No sir, sausage, on account of it's a sausage roll,' Carmel explains. 'Bloody Americans, want jam on everything.' She turns to Flora, 'We were just saying about Holly being, youknow, what David said.'

'And I am,' I added, 'I certainly am.'

'Well,' says Flora vaguely, 'yes. That's 75 pence that salad, love. Shocking isn't it, prices they pay. We've only got the crackers for 20 pence, sweetheart. Ask Mummy for another 20 and I'll get you a scone and butter. Well men don't understand do they? I used to have a friend. Still write to her even now and it's been seven years. "My dear Florrie" she says, only one to call me 'Florrie'. Emigrated to South Africa, ooh I was upset. My eyes were that red and puffy, people kept asking me had I had a fight with my old man.'

'What kind of pate do you have?'

'Meat,' says Carmel firmly, 'meat pate. Which one is it?' she asks me, 'Your friend I mean, is it the one you went to the airport with?'

'And the quiche? What's in the quiche?'

'Red pepper,' I say, squinting vaguely at bits of tomato. 'Yes, she was going to her son's wedding.'

'Oh,' says Flora, 'I thought it was the one come in here the other night. She out of favour then, poor girl?'

'Do you miss her?' asks Carmel, 'if she's gone to America. Spect you miss her.'

'Course she does,' says Flora. 'I've already rung up the till, love, so I'll have to add the two trays together. How long's she gone for?'

'Two weeks.'

'Oh well,' says Carmel.

'How long've you had?' asks Flora.

'A month and three days.'

'I should write to her,' says Flora. 'Tonight, when you get in. Write her a nice long letter.'

'Yes,' says Carmel, unwrapping more tea bags and stacking them in cups, 'people like letters. Don't say about being lonely and missing her and all, in case she thinks you're moping.'

'I am moping,' I say.

'Just tell her what you been doing,' says Carmel, 'make her miss you.' "

Five: Flora

"I've been working here twenty five years, brought the till with me when we moved in seventy three. Half the money keeps this place going comes through my cash desk, and do you know, I've never had a chair? Sposed to take a break instead. Fat chance. Said they'd get me a swivel in the end, being as I'm so small. That was six months ago. Carmel got me a stool from the bar just the right height, only Jonathan said it wasn't on, cos it obscures the price list we're legally bound to display. And me with my veins. It's the arthritis is worse, only I don't like to mention that. Jonathan keeps on at me to transfer to Accounts, but that's only a day job and who'd pop into my mother's? It's a way to get rid of me really. Still, don't complain till you're sure you'll win, otherwise they'll do it harder, as my mum says. I park me bum on the counter and let the girls keep a look out when we're not busy.

'There he is!' said Carmel, 'Holly look up the security number. He knows he's not to come in here.'

The TV was in again. Pink June, we call him, don't know why, one of the ushers started it and it just stuck. He goes round the tables drinking left over slops like a potboy, eating other people's pastry crust. Harmless really, and he cheers up the security, gives them something to do. Wears a long pink floaty dress with lots of layers and a scarf in his hair. He'd look old-fashioned if he wasn't so dirty. Always the same dress. Plucks his legs with a tweezer, someone should tell him about ladyshaves, that's what my daughter uses. The ushers say there's a lot of complaints: men take them aside and warn them about a woman washing out her smalls in the Gents; women say there's a man, least they think it's a man, using the Ladies' Cloakroom. Well, I draw the line at that. He's still a man, for all he wears a dress, and young Holly gets changed in there. He might ask her to zip him up. Security say it's a disgrace he's allowed in the building, wouldn't want to bring your old mother here with that sort of thing going on. I tell you, I have other worries for my mother. I worry she'll electrocute herself, mistake the bleach for the thermos; I worry I'll take after her, that I won't take after her enough.

'Why not have your tea now?' said Carmel, 'While the

23

queue's died down.' Lucky they made her manageress, if we had to wait for Jonathan, we'd never get off.

'I'll just have a fag and sit out at one of the tables,' I said, 'can't be bothered traipsing up them stairs.'

Two flights, and the lift never comes, and I can't eat half the food in the canteen cos of my stomach. Though you're not really sposed to sit with the customers.

Only table free had Pink June scavenging it, well he wasn't a customer.

'Do sit down, my dear,' he said.

So I did. Wasn't anywhere else.

'I've been admiring your bow,' he said.

It's part of the uniform. Me and Holly do ours in a tie. Carmel wears hers in a bow.

'And the stockings. A perfect match. Purple is so elegant.'

I'm a more than middle-aged lady, I've got varicose veins that hurt on account of I've been standing for the last twenty five years. Purple tights can only make my legs look that much lumpier, uglier, and because they are tight, more painful. I looked at them now, couldn't help it. Pink June looked too. Terrible twisted knots that stand out so I can't bear to have my daughter's child run up against them, thick roundness at my knees, swollen with arthritis. I thought about my mother's legs, only twenty years older than mine, blotchy with brown and blue patches, fat at the bottom as though all the flesh had slipped down into her shoes. My legs are not elegant. A living testament, a warning to others, perhaps. Elegant, no. Pink June had moved on, found half a doughnut somewhere. God but he is disgusting. I waited through that pain you get in the small of your back when you first sit down after you been used to standing. I get pins and needles in my feet when I sit down. I wonder sometimes if I'll end up like a cow and sleep on my legs too. I hid them under the table, so I couldn't think about it any more, and lit a fag.

'Ah,' said a voice, 'the lady with the light.'

Pink June. Still prancing about more ladylike than thou. I lit his cigarette for him. He was holding it with the very tips of his fingers; tilted his chin, flashed a bony profile, then breathed smoke at the spotlight. His face was powdery with make-up.

My mum wears a lot of make-up. Not eye shadow or mascara but powder, always, bit of rouge and a bit of lipstick. 'I may be half dead, but I don't have to look it.' I have to buy the exact same kind each time, otherwise she don't recognise the shape. Be surprised how quickly the brands change. She could put the stuff on in the dark; that's not the problem. Been doing it more than sixty years, so she knows the shape of her face.

'Oh disaster!' squeaked Pink June suddenly, standing right behind me. 'Do have a look for me, dear, and tell me have I smudged my lipstick?'

So I looked at him and I wanted to break his jaw. He was revelling in it. Sneering at us. Carmel leaves her kids off at my place when she goes Keep Fit. It's a handful with my mother and two toddlers, but we manage. One time when the kids were there, we went shopping. Ran out of coffee, well my mother said she'd grin and bear it, and maybe Carmel could bring some back with her, but I wanted to get out for a bit anyway. Mum got into her chair, and we settled Liam on her knee, sideways so as not to jar her back. I fixed the trolley basket to the handles, told Michelle to hold on, and we set off. We were fine going down in the lift, and the kids behaved themselves. I think we all felt very enterprising, like Crackerjack when you get prizes for how many cabbages you can hold in your arms at one time.

We got as far as the bus stop without mishap. I had no idea how I was going to get both kids, my mother, the wheelchair and the shopping trolley all onto the bus. The adventure'd worn off. Mum said Liam was getting heavy, Michelle was tired of walking, and I wanted someone to carry me. Course, as a mother you're meant to plan everything beforehand, every step. But sometimes you can't be bothered; want to wheel the problem out into the street so everyone can trip over it.

Well, the bus stopped and there was a woman on the platform waiting to jump off. She helped lift Liam and Michelle up and passed them down inside the bus to the other passengers. Then my mother clambered on. It's quite a step for her, but she hadn't been out for ages. Finally I folded the wheelchair and stowed it with the trolley under the stairs. The conductor came down then, wondering what was the hold-up. 'Whose is this trolley?' he started to shout,

'Can't have a trolley and a wheelchair. No room.' 'Course there's room,' my mother protested. 'There's loads of room.' 'Sorry Missis, regulations. What if they was to fall out?' 'Well you'll have to keep an eye on them,' said my mother. The conductor was going to say a whole lot more, but he could see the disapproval rising in the bus so he just snarled a 'Look after it yourself, not my job.' 'Thank you, young man,' smiled my mother, 'it's very kind of you.' He looked at her then and winked. 'Wouldn't do it for all the girls, you know. Only the pretty ones.'

I'm sorry, did I say I wanted to smash Pink June's jaw? I was wrong. I want to run him over with a wheelchair, a double buggy and a shopping trolley full of tins of cat food. I want to teach him to smile at men for the smallest courtesies, to paint his face or lose his job.

'Where's Flora now?' Jonathan asked Carmel irritably. 'She knows she's not to sit with the customers.'

'Only gone to the loo,' retorted Carmel.

'Bloody old bat's always powdering her nose. She incontinent or what?' "

Six: Carmel

"Night Valerie, see you tomorrow," Holly called out.

"You'll see her in ten minutes," said Carmel.

"How come?"

"She's only gone to change."

"Won't take that long."

"Will with what she's squeezing into."

"How do you mean?"

"For the party. There's a Showcase party on tonight. Everyone's invited."

"First I've heard of it."

"Oh it was your night off yesterday, sure enough. Well you could still go. Don't have to dress up."

"Ner. Won't be any of my sort there."

"Look, there's Jackie and her sister. She's only fifteen.

26

Looks older, doesn't she? Come on over here to the counter, Jack. You look gorgeous. Really gorgeous."

"Blimey, Jack, how dyou get into those red pants? They're skin tight."

Soon Jackie, Debbie, Valerie and the others were parading in front of the counter, inches taller and much brighter in the face than their normal work gear.

"Oh don't you look a picture," said Flora.

"Come on," said Jackie, "we'd better buy some booze. And you needn't think you're getting any," she added to the little sister. "You lot sure you're not coming?"

"Go on, Carmel," Val urged her, "you're all eager."

"No," said Carmel, sitting down to make the point. "I'm a happily married mother of two."

"And I'm pushing sixty," said Flora, perching on the counter.

"And I'm a dyke," said Holly simply, leaning against the coffee machine.

"Well," said Carmel roundly, when the others had gone, "I think I'll just suck a lemon."

"Do what?"

"For my diet. Citrus fruit. Burns up the fat. Do you know Jackie thinks she's fat? And did you see her in those red pants? Skin tight they were. Skin, skinny tight."

"Jackie's really pretty," said Holly, "that red just suits her brown skin."

"Why don't you suck an orange?" asked Flora, "Much nicer."

"My husband's always on at me to lose weight."

"Or a grapefruit," said Holly.

"It's only cause he's proud of me."

"Or a peach," said Flora.

"He even notices when I haven't polished my toenails."

"Or a nectarine," said Holly.

"What's that?" asked Carmel.

"Pure nectar," said Holly, "cross between a peach and a plum. Yum, yum."

"Never tasted one," said Carmel.

"Got some in my bag," said Holly.

So while the others swanned off to the party, and Val got off with the security guard, and Jackie's trousers split, and the little sister got so pissed she had to be taken home, and they all left in Debbie's father's taxi, Holly, Carmel and Flora were biting into the soft, sweet flesh of the fruit and letting its sticky juice run down their chins.

"So that was a nectarine," said Carmel, "next time someone compares me to one, I'll know what they're talking about."

"Well lets hope she doesn't spit you out like that pip," laughed Holly.

"She?" repeated Carmel, "Chance'd be a fine thing. More likely to be my barmy husband. Be a relief if he saw me as a nectarine, usually he thinks I'm Princess Margaret and all sorts."

"He's off again, is he?" asked Flora sympathetically.

"He is," said Carmel, "last week it was the English out to get us; this week it's the Provos. Kicks with both feet, that one."

"And are they?" asked Flora.

"Don't be silly," said Holly, "Carmel's not a terrorist."

"It's not silly," said Carmel, "daft maybe, but not silly."

"Well that's the thing," said Flora, "it's cos he's scared himself. You think he's tormenting you, but he thinks it's protection."

"Perhaps he thinks it's good for you to be scared," suggested Holly.

"I think he thinks it's good for him," retorted Carmel, "last week he had me and the kids on the floor in our dressing gowns. This time he comes to me with this story how it's not safe for me out on my own alone and I must stop in till he can drive me in the car. I've no patience with it."

"But it's probably true," said Flora. "What about those men you said about on the tube after all the Irish stuff last week?"

"It's funny," said Holly, "I never think of you as Irish. I mean I know you are, because of your name and accent, but . ."

"If I only tried a little harder I could get rid of that?" said Carmel. "You know when I go over home they say I've an English accent. 'You're anti- anti- Irish', says my Dad, 'You only lose it if you want to lose it.' 'How did we come to produce two little cockneys?' says Peg, my husband's mother, when the kids are out playing. Then my husband comes to me with this story how Mick's lot are after me. I was at school with Mick and we went out together, till he got involved with the funny crowd. He was a nice boy and he had a motor bike, but what with him going away on weekends, and Sean the drummer walking into my life, we didn't last very long. A year after we split, Mick got put away for shooting some fellow, so that was that. Cept my husband has it all figured out how Mick's lot think it was me put him inside, and have some contract out on me, and how I have to lay low till we can sneak back to Ireland and get Peg to make them leave off, and she'd do that for me because she's a soft spot since I taught her to type last long boring holidays we were over and I'd nothing better to do, and then she'd speak to her husband on her bended knee, and he's the biggest man in County Cork so of course they'd listen to him."

"Would they?" asked Flora.

"Mick's been inside ten years now," said Carmel, "my husband just doesn't want me out of his sight."

"Besides," said Holly, "Mick was your boyfriend, you went to school with those blokes."

"If they wanted to, they'd do it," said Carmel, "Jack was shot in the back last year for being in the wrong street."

"Jesus!" said Holly.

"What I want," said Carmel, "is one day to walk, just walk, not anywhere in particular, just on my own without any of my husband's warnings what might happen if I'm not entirely entrusted to his protection."

"Wish I had your guts," said Flora.

"Could do with them myself," said Carmel, "only with my husband you lose your sense of proportion. Thing is, you see, they are out to get me. He just keeps getting it wrong who."

Seven: Holly

"Jonathan wants you," said Carmel before Holly'd had time to take her coat off, "upstairs."

"What's he want?" asked Holly. There were only two things you saw Jonathan upstairs for: to get your contract and to get your cards. It was so long since Holly'd signed her contract, she doubted she'd even remember the office number.

"Best go now, love," said Flora, "you'll worry either way." As Holly walked towards the lift she went over all the misdemeanours she could be sacked for. Had security seen her with those avocados? But shit, Carmel was always passing them pieces of melon, didn't that keep them sweet? Maybe the till was out and they thought it was her. That was easy to prove. Flora wouldn't let anyone near it, even for change for the phone. Eating in front of the customers? Surely not. Oh Christ! That customer she'd told to f off, the posh old bloke who kept asking were they open because, though he had his coffee and his game pie, the women chatted to each other while they served him. He must be Jonathan's boyfriend. Must be, bound to be. Same twitch of the nose as though no hanky could ever be soft enough; same air of thinking women had better things to do in this world than talk amongst themselves. Holly would tell Jonathan she was sorry, would apologise for Carmel too, say that Carmel's daughter had whooping cough and she was scared she'd have a convulsion. By the time she reached the seventh floor and was knocking politely on Jonathan's door, Holly had her whole story figured out.

A blue light labelled 'wait' lit up. Holly waited. Presently Mrs Guthrie, Jonathan's secretary, appeared, showing a young man out.

"If you don't mind stepping outside for a few minutes," she was saying, "I have to see this young lady. Come along in dear."

Holly came.

"Now sit yourself down." Mrs Guthrie pointed towards a chair the other side of the room from her desk. Obviously not a cosy chat. Mrs Guthrie didn't sit; she toyed nervously with her pearls and perched uncomfortably on the side of her desk.

"Well now," she said with an awkward smile, "this is embarrassing."

Holly could see it was embarrassing. Mrs Guthrie was fidgeting with her pearls.

"Jonathan asked me to speak to you . . ."

Couldn't even do his own dirty work.

"He's heard from the people you work with that you have a problem with . . ."

Holly sweated. The words were such a long time coming. She was torn between pity for Mrs Guthrie and the awful thing she had to say, and pity for herself and what she was going to have to hear.

"You have a problem with B.O.," Mrs Guthrie finished miserably.

"B.O.?" Holly repeated, too stunned to react, "You mean I'm dirty?"

"Oh no! Not dirty!" said Mrs Guthrie.

"You mean I smell?"

"I wondered if perhaps you didn't have enough blouses," Mrs Guthrie suggested limply. "This is terrible," she added almost as an aside, "like telling someone they eat too much garlic." However, she pulled herself together sufficiently to continue. "He said it was very difficult, what with the food and all, you do understand?"

Holly understood. Jonathan was summing her up: You have hairs on your legs, he was saying, and under your arms. Your breasts are unbound. You walk in the foyer of the Nation's Showcase holding hands with a woman, whom you then kiss. So really, you know, you must smell.

"I'll leave it with you then," said Mrs Guthrie, twiddling manically with her pearls.

"Yes," said Holly, "you leave it with me." And she walked back to the lift. She pressed the button for the ground floor. 'He's heard from the people you work with' echoed again and again, till it seemed to boom up and down the lift shaft. This was not the first time she had been sacked for making her sexuality more than a saucy question mark, but did it have to be Carmel and Flora who dobbed her in? Carmel who'd eaten her nectarine; Flora who advised her to write a nice letter. Couldn't Jonathan have left her to believe he'd seen her himself with Ruth on one of his rare visits to the ground floor?

Eight: Flora

"Well love?" asked Flora, as soon as Holly got to the counter.

"Oh it was ridiculous," said Holly, laughing already herself to give the others their cue, determined not to show how much they'd hurt her. "Making me go all the way up there just to tell me that. He could have left me a note. Made Mrs Guthrie do it too, couldn't face me himself."

"What did she say?" asked Carmel.

"Trying to get me to leave of my own accord so he doesn't have to sack me," Holly continued.

"What did he say?" asked Flora.

"Needn't have bothered. I want shut of this job anyway. The way people talk about you behind your back."

"What's that supposed to mean?" snapped Carmel.

"He said you told him I stink," said Holly. The words seemed to burst out despite her.

"What?"

"You heard me."

"And you believed him?"

"Well did you? Did you say that?" It was the only way Holly could get her own back, by throwing Jonathan's accusation in their faces. Though the slur would still stick. Be all over the building. How Holly got the sack cos she smelt so bad. Did she fart a lot or did she have a Problem? Imagine that on your reference.

"You think we stand here, all chatting together, and as soon as you go off on your break, we go on about how you smell?" said Carmel.

"Do you?" pleaded Holly, wondering at the breaking note in her own voice.

"No, sweetheart," said Flora, looking shocked, "Jonathan's made it all up."

"He's a nasty piece of work," said Carmel, "if Flora goes off to the loo he says she's incontinent."

"What did you say?" asked Flora, horrified, "he says what?"

"Flora, the man's a complete pig. Makes me wonder what's his noble estimation of me. Carmel, the dirty, drunken, stupid, Irish slut. Brain probably rotten with

32

potcheen and potato blight."

"He wants to move me to Accounts," said Flora, "nice little part time day job. Know what that means, don't you? Licking labels and franking envelopes. Only cos they can't sack me. Been here longer than any of them. Know what it is though, we get on too well together, the three of us, and they don't like that. Say I'm making too many mistakes on my till."

"Oh Flora," said Holly, "tell them it's me and Carmel. Say we take over on your breaks and keep ringing up wrong."

"No," sighed Flora, "he knows I don't take breaks. Can't face the stairs. (Pause). I wouldn't mind a desk job really."

"Mean you'd get a chair after all these years."

"Think of that. And I'm only two years off retirement."

"Then you get a gold watch," said Holly.

"It's not really a gold watch I'm after," said Flora with a sudden gleam.

"Oh yeah, what you got your beady eye on, so?"

"Well . . ."

"Go on tell us," said Holly, "we could have a whip round."

"You see it's me mum and the kettle . . ."

"You want a new one?"

"No o o."

"Teasmade?"

"My mum don't drink tea."

"Coffee pot?"

Carmel looked around.

"Jesus you've some cheek. Oooh the cold, brass, brazen cheek of it."

"What?" asked Holly, then added admiringly, "Blimey! But how the hell do we get it out of here?"

To the annoyance and frustration of a thirsty public visiting the Nation's Showcase, the coffee machine in the main foyer broke down in the middle of the interval. Carmel had to ring the engineer, but it was no good, without the little plastic plug and chain weighting down the lever which completed the electric circuit, there was no way he could fix it. The plug, which must have disappeared while Holly was emptying the coffee slops, was a safety device. It sat at the bottom of the slop tray and if the machine flooded, the plug would float, the chain slacken and release the lever, cutting off the circuit before anyone could electrocute herself. Carmel asked the engineer what on earth she, as manageress, could do, for neither David nor Jonathan, her supervisors, were anywhere to be found (unless she sent to the bar, which was of course the last place one would think of). The engineer said there was an old machine up in the buffet, she should get security to bring it down in the goods lift and take the faulty one out. They might as well leave it in the foyer for tonight, no one would exactly walk off with it.

The switch was effected in but a moment and the public impressed with such a speedy response to calamity. Nothing tastes better than the cup of coffee you were very nearly deprived of. The night was otherwise uneventful. Pink June came in again and the security chased him round the underground car park. The women didn't mind dealing with the broken machine themselves for, though it was heavy, it was at least on casters. David stumbled into it and demanded that such an obstacle be removed before someone broke their neck and sued. At about ten o'clock Carmel suggested closing, as there were few customers left.

"Who's duty manager?" asked Flora.

"Mrs Guthrie," said Holly. "But don't worry," she added, thinking of the agitated fingers with the pearl necklace, "I'm sure she'll turn a blind eye."

Carmel's husband arrived to fetch her as usual and was persuaded to give everyone a lift home in his dry cleaning van. The coffee machine squeaked happily on its little casters as it ambled up the ramp.

"It won't be the same without you," said Carmel while her husband obligingly rigged up the machine.

"I'll only be in Accounts," said Flora. "And I'll be popping in for the refills."

"No, no, no," came her mother's voice from the kitchen, "there's that stand pipe there for a washing machine. Only I don't have a washing machine. Do all my wash by hand cos the water goes such a lovely colour. Deep purple brown, wouldn't miss it for the world though I am seventy eight years old. Well you can stick that tube off the end of that for the water, can't you. I'd do it myself, only I seem to have company."

"Well, Mrs Carroll," said Holly when the woman finally appeared, "and how do you like your new coffee pot?"

Mrs Carroll paused a while to consider. "Nice. It's very nice, dear, and I like the smell of those coffee beans. Gives you hope somehow. But," and she directed her next remark towards her daughter, "it's not quite like Greek coffee in real Greek sunshine."

"I know, Mum, I know," sighed Flora, "but I couldn't keep it up."

"Never mind, dear," said her mother, "I counted up the tips box and there's enough in there for an off-season Marbella."

"Tips?" repeated Holly, "Don't tell me the customers show their appreciation."

"In this world," said Mrs Carroll severely, "you got to learn to appreciate yourself."

Nine: Carmel

Monday evening Carmel was late for work. Plus she was on her own. On her own except for Katie, the student, that is and it's well known that students never think of any job as work, something they have to do. Minds on higher things; read their books because they're bored and don't check the machines are full. And for all they're so clever, they won't do anything they're not told to: when the meat safes drip they talk about convection, they don't empty the troughs. Get to know them a bit and they're off back to university. Carmel spent her life showing other people how to do their jobs.

"So why did the last girl leave?" asked Katie bouncily.

"What's it to you?" snapped Carmel.

"Oh I don't know, just chatting."

"Look if it's small talk you're after, could you pick something small?"

"I was only asking. Don't have to bite my head off. Start a new job, you want to know what happened to your predecessor."

"Do you?" asked Carmel, "Well Flora was past it and Holly's a queer. Alright?"

"Oh that's terrible," gasped Katie, "didn't think they sacked people for being homosexual these days."

"They didn't sack her. She left."

"I don't understand that," said Katie, "did she get a chip on her shoulder?"

"Why're you bothered? Got the job didn't you?" said Carmel, adding impatiently, "And if you want to keep it you'd better at least starting filling up those shelves, or David'll be over asking why not."

As Carmel wrote out the stock sheets, she wondered why Katie expected to understand. Expected things written out neat and clear for her, like how to use a library catalogue. And why couldn't Holly have weathered it? Jonathan would get over his fit, Mrs Guthrie might even apologise. And if Flora had battled it out with the union . . . But it wasn't that. Dirty and incontinent, they were terrible words. Carmel stabbed viciously at the passion cake. The only nice thing about this lousy fucking job was that she and the others had a bit of a chat, a good crack sometimes.

No one had yet appeared to replace Flora, so for the next few hours Carmel was on the till. First off she got two orange crates and arranged them to sit on, thinking the while of how Flora used to rub her knees with her swollen knuckles, wondering how she had stood it for so long. Nearly sixty, praps she was doting already like Jonathan said. And Holly, well you never knew, did you? It was a small space to work in. Made you feel funny to think of her hands on you. Not that she ever did. Carmel shuddered. Was that what people thought about Holly, whenever she told them?

That morning Carmel's husband had a bit of a discharge. Carmel hadn't noticed anything on herself, except maybe a pimple. But they were both so scared of that sort of thing that Carmel had written down the name of a Special Clinic from a toilet wall and said they must make an appointment. Only her husband, who knew more about it, said they'd put this wire loop right down the middle of his thing, which hurts like hell, and couldn't she go, as they always gave you something for your partner as well, if the test was positive.

So Carmel went. Filled out the form and waited.

"Carmel Byrne," said the Doctor, reading out what she'd written, "born in Cork City. So you're one of the little people are you?"

His stage Irish accent surprised her. She hadn't thought Doctors were that ignorant.

"I'm Irish," she said simply. Hoping her simplicity would disarm him.

"Takes all sorts," he said smiling. "I'm a little absent minded meself."

Carmel didn't get the joke, though it took an awful effort.

"So you think you may have contracted a venereal disease?" he continued, reaching for his public school accent. "Well, lets examine you."

And for the next hour there were blood tests and urine tests, surgical gloves and cervical scrapes, sitting half-dressed in waiting rooms interspersed with:

"Not the first time we've seen you in here, is it Miss Byrne?"

"You do have running water in your house?"

"This leaflet here has very clear diagrams, in case you get into trouble with the print."

At one point Carmel was called off into a side room and asked to read letters off a card, told to cover one ear and locate the direction of a particular sound. Were they always this thorough? she wondered, what could these tests discover that a blood sample would not? They must think her so riddled with syph that her eyesight was failing her! Finally the Doctor told her:

"You have venereal warts. Do you indulge in anal intercourse?"

"No."

"Are you sure?"

"Sure? What's there to be sure about? You think I might not have noticed?"

The Doctor sniffed. "At all events apply four drops of this liquid to each growth. It may sting a little. Come back and see me in three weeks time."

Carmel left the clinic swearing never to go back for the rest of her life, and if that was where you ended up, she'd swear off sex as well. She was only glad there was a separate exit from the rear of the hospital so she could sneak quietly up the steps and away. No wonder no one ever spoke of it. How could you admit to being in a place like that? Had any of her friends had to go there? And was that what they said to them? Did she have running water! What kind of a question was that? And he didn't even believe her when she told him she didn't go in for that funny business. Whatever did he think of her?

Any defences Carmel might have built up against knowing exactly what the Doctor thought of her were swept away by the first application of the drops he'd given her. He'd said they would sting a little; in fact they burned, burned red hot in that sensitive area so that, when she went to dab herself with a little water, she saw that her pants were smeared red with blood. And she knew that the liquid he'd given her was far too concentrated, and she knew that she knew this, and that he was punishing her, first of all for being Irish, then for not laughing at herself with him, and finally for making him feel he'd been racist.

So Flora was going to slump into a badly paid day job, in a place which owed twenty five years of her life. And what chance had Holly of finding anything else in catering with the references Jonathan would give her?

"Did she have anything lined up?" It was Katie again.

"Who?" asked Carmel crossly, thinking of the series of assistants who might come and go. Holly was not so easily forgotten that Carmel would open her heart to Katie.

"Well either," pursued Katie, "that Jonathan seemed a right slimey toad."

"In your considered opinion," sneered Carmel.

"He told me I'm too young and I only got the job because two of them walked out."

"We all have our cross to bear."

"So what happened? And why're you taking it out on me?"

"Well," said Carmel finally, wondering how much she could tell of each story, "I don't want you to think it was all terrible, we had a good crack sometimes."

1 WOMAN = 7 CUPS OF TEA

Wednesday 30th March 1983

Dear Hester,

Blimey O'Reilly, whoever would have thought it and you'll never guess what. On Tuesday night, twenty ninth of March nineteen eighty three (yesterday, to be precise) yours truly found herself in bed, body for body, with the illustrious Elsie Hooper. You know, the one I gaze at from behind the Accounts Book at Collective meetings (ooh that lazy mouth of hers), the one who always rushes in late and can never stay to go down the pub (and those long fingers which positively drip into the Minutes), who we all decided had a jealous lover and a long piece of string, (and the way she slouches, crouches like a coiled spring in my wicker chair. My wicked chair.) With this Elsie, then, I slept, last night, and the following day, this very morning, was gratified to find on my pillow, after she'd gone, a love letter, or, more prosaically, a thank you note. You will incline towards the latter description, I hold for the former. But I have copied the note she wrote me (oh the little flutter that afflicts the heart, while the hand writes and the mind memorises the words of the loved and lusted) and enclose it for your perusal.

The circumstances of our meeting were thus:

I had met Maeve for a Lebanese at Earl's Court, and was returning home on the District Line. It was about 9pm. I was standing on the platform and my heart was churning, for it had just then occurred to me that I might, that it was just possible I might, meet the illustrious Elsie. She works as a cashier or something at the Exhibition Centre – a circumstance which had not entirely escaped me when I suggested to Maeve that we eat there. I felt pretty flash: was wearing my tight turquoise jeans and wondering at what angle to tilt my peacock beret, imagining that at any moment Elsie might appear from the crowd, might nod in my direction, might smile and say hello. A nod from Elsie! A smile! We might even, if the carriage were not too crowded, if she too were a non-smoker – I rather thought she was – travel part of the way together, sit next to each other, have a conversation. Like the proud mother with a list of her baby's first words, I could remember almost everything that Elsie had said to me, and almost all I had replied as she hurried to find a seat and direct the Collective meeting.

Now I began to stare at the faces of the crowd, searching for traces of Elsie: young women with headphones mouthing the lyrics of soundless songs; two Australians eating oranges on a bench. This one had her lazy mouth, that one her slouch. Sometimes I really thought I saw her coming towards me. I closed my eyes, concentrated, traced every line of her face and then, when I thought I had every shadow, every curve, I looked up and willed her to stand in front of me. Such a crowd coming out of the Ideal Homes tunnel. So many people who weren't Elsie.

Then my train pulled in and it would not have done to get too carried away. As you said on Friday, Elsie's this week, next week it'll be someone else: Maeve perhaps or even you, Hester, if I didn't know you too well to leave room for fantasies. It's just that Elsie's so bright, so venomous, a challenge worth rising to. But I wanted to meet her somewhere ordinary, somewhere she didn't have all the power. Such was the run of my thoughts, when I wandered onto the train, that I did not at first notice I was in a smoking compartment. Spurning the interconnecting doors, which would have made me feel like a skinhead, I waited till the tube stopped to change carriages.

There was an odd atmosphere as I entered. You know, polite avoidance, as though someone had been quietly sick. Two women in mauve wool gazed with concern at a sleeping figure in the seat opposite.

"Do you think she's alright?"

"Asleep probably."

"Praps we should tell someone."

"She wouldn't thank you."

The figure was slumped and its head swayed with the vibrations of the train. It had blue circles round its eyes and its shoes twitched. A navy shirt and a tabard. A uniform of some kind. It's funny the way one often doesn't see a person in a uniform. One expects it to be cleaning something and it seems more tactful to pretend one hasn't noticed. This woman was asleep. Well, either she was asleep, the sleep of ten hours a day, six days a week, clock out of work and collapse or... The tube sped round a corner, the lights flickered, the sleeper's foot twitched.

"Praps we should wake her up. Wouldn't want to miss her stop."

"You're not in Sheffield now, Barbara. Best leave well alone."

"Not very well," I thought to myself, staring at the sleeping woman. Though I don't suppose I'd have given her a second thought if the other two hadn't been anxious. People are always collapsing, it is better not to interfere if you have any kind of life to live yourself. The figure shifted slightly. Blue circles, crimplene skirt, dirty tabard: it was Elsie.

Elsie Hooper! Elsie who was so funny, so irritating, who could make even Maeve shut up and listen. Elsie with her face marked a furious red from the armrest, her pillow. Elsie crouching at a meeting ready to pounce. Elsie twitching, shuffling.

"It's alright," I said to the women in mauve wool, "she's a friend of mine."

"There you are," one said to the other, smiling roundly, finally able to sit comfortable and open her nice book.

I sat down next to Elsie. She's always so articulate, 'raucous with rhetoric' as you put it, and I'd imagined, I spose because she's that much older than me, in my fantasies of the first kiss, that she would sweep me off my feet. At the moment she didn't look much like she could sweep a jacket potato into a rubbish bag.

What I felt then, on seeing my idol thus fallen, was acutely disappointed and somewhat aggrieved. I wanted a brilliant, witty, slightly vicious idol with a lazy mouth who would keep me on my feet, not yet-another-tired-feminist I would have to look after. But it passed quickly. She opened her eyes blearily as I sat down and asked dimly from the armrest:

"What station is it?"

"Victoria. Just pulling out."

"Pulling out?" she squeaked, "It can't. It can't do that. It's my stop." She jerked awake and stared dismally at the closed doors, the slowly disappearing blue tiles, lacking even the energy of a trapped bird as it bangs its head against the glass. Then she started to cry.

"I can't bear it," she sobbed softly, "I don't know what I'm going to do." She slouched back in her seat, a movement I recognised, though there seemed no spring in her now. Then, squeezing a last trickle of steel, she said, as though reciting a poem:

"I shall go on to Embankment. I shall change there for the Northern Line. The connection is quite quick. I shall close my eyes for two more stations. I shall remember to wake up."

"Elsie," I broke in tenderly, "next stop's Saint James's. Come home with me."

For once I was pleased to live in the West End. Normally it meant at least six stations to a decent lesbian life.

"Come on," I repeated, "up the escalator, hand in your ticket, cross the zebra and we're home."

Elsie muttered something about an imposition, but she shambled to her feet anyway, gathering her bags to her like a tramp. I'd eaten already with Maeve, but I put the pan on the stove for her, and she watched with a glazed look while I chopped, sprinkled and fried.

"Salt and pepper on that table there," she mumbled, "and don't spill it cos it's me's got to clear it up."

Suddenly she jumped up and said:

"No! You can't wait on me. It's not right. It's servicing, pandering."

She took hold of the frying pan and began to stir it with a tea spoon. The spoon must have felt too light in her hand, for she looked at it suspiciously and shook it a few times, like an unfurled umbrella. Poor little love. I was wracked with pity but I daren't be effusive.

"Oh Sonya," she said flopping down again, starting to cry again, "they've taken my brain away and replaced it with multiples of five."

"Would you like a cup of tea?" I tried.

"Milk? Sugar? That'll be 25 pence please."

I stared at her.

"That's what I mean," she said, "ten hours a day I talk to my till. It's a voluble and demanding conversationalist, but its vocabulary is unfortunately limited. Did you know, if you count in fives from nought to a hundred, the sum of the figures equals one thousand and fifty? It suddenly came to me one day when I was adding one sausage roll, one cheese and tomato, one egg and cress; but there was no one to tell and the till knew already. All I see are the numbers on the cash register, I daren't look at the people for fear there was a pile up and someone fell off. Like eggs on a conveyor belt."

Once started, it all seeemd to come out in a rush.

"When my supervisor comes to relieve me, I have a go cleaning tables. Then at least my brain isn't chained. But people are so possessive about their rubbish – little deaths throughout the day: their soggy tissues, their spilled ash trays. I raise their tin foil sandwich wrappers as carefully as a mother her baby's bottom."

"Bring out your dead."

"Any rubbish?"

"Only my husband."

"Have you done yet?"

"Have you come yet?"

"Can I wipe it all away now?"

"Would you just give this table a flick love?"

"Would you just give my prick a suck love?"

"I daren't look at the people."

"The crumbs of your sausage roll in the pink palm of her hands."

"Could do with one of you in my ideal home, love."

"And you know what?" said Elsie, "A cup of tea costs 25 pence. They give me £1.75 an hour. 1 woman equals 7 cups of tea."

"A woman is worth seven cups of tea," I thought.

Elsie had stopped crying. I hoped it was because she felt better. I placed a plate of dahl in front of her, but her head slipped from its resting place on her hand and fell into the lentils. I picked her up, put her arm round my shoulder and dragged her off to bed. I undressed her and returned shortly with a hot water bottle, lovingly wrapped in my maroon cashmere sweater for fear of scalding her toes. She went out like a light. Like a table cleaner. Like a cashier.

I washed up and watched telly. There was nothing much on. I thought about Elsie, about jobs, about women and cups of tea. Not that 'life creates waste' but that it generates desire, and the safest bromide is pity. They put bromide in the tea in men's prisons. A woman is worth seven cups of tea. I was so sorry for Elsie I couldn't feel sexual. Uppermost in my mind came duty, next down a formless anger that fatigue had placed her beyond response. Then I went to bed myself. I undressed in the dark and fumbled my way to the left of the bed. Normally I sleep the other side, as there is nowhere to put the glass of water or the reading lamp. For a while I lay awake, wondering what I would tell you, for here I was sleeping with the illustrious Ell, and there she was, snoring her way through my epic moment. I dozed off musing about Maeve.

At 8.30 next morning, like every morning, I woke up. My five year clock sees to that. I lay still a moment with the distinct feeling that Something had happened the night before, though I could not yet think what. I turned my head on the pillow and realised instantly that Someone Else had slept there with me, or I would not now find myself on the left. A pick up at a disco? Didn't think I went in for that. An old friend staying over? I wondered whether it had been good: had I come or got scared? In the next few thoughts I realised that whoever it was had now gone, and then that they had left a note. I unfolded it. This is what it said:

"You are as beautiful as 4 sandwiches and 8 teas which cost exactly five pounds when I have no change in my till.

You are as beautiful as a butter wrapper neatly folded so my hands don't get greasy when I clear up.

You are as beautiful as the woman who left Sheffield at 3.30 in the morning and did not throw her tea slops in my bin liner.

44

You are as beautiful as the squashed cream slice a
customer returned and I ate.

You are as beautiful as the dirty soup bowl under the sink
which will complete my 36 piece dinner service.

Sonya,
Not the broken chair I hide behind the trolley to sit on,

Not the bomb scare that clears the building in five
minutes,

Not my clock card at home time is more beautiful than
you.

Love and Thanks,
Elsie."

So tell me, Hester, is this a thank you note or a love letter?
Is she after my body or does she want a nice cup of tea?

Yours truly,

Sonya.

MIND THE GAP

"Mind the gap.
Mind the gap.
Will lesbians please mind the gap
and stand clear of the doors."

"I don't believe it," said Monica, "I refuse to believe it. I refuse to believe I am sitting here with a pint of Young's in my outstretched hand, down The Railway, which is my local, and where I mostly find myself come nine o'clock, sitting next to Rachel, who is my closest friend, and has been for the last six years, our backs to the wall, staring vaguely out at the other customers, lefties for the most part though fewer since the boycott, and that I am saying, or rather that I am whining,

'Why Rachel? Tell me why not?'
and that she is taking a deep breath, and heaving a sigh at the same time, which rather spoils the effect, because it looks like she's doing breathing exercises, blowing her hair out of her eyes in that familiar way she has, even though it has been short for six months now; that she starts off by saying

'Because,'
but, finding it all too much for her, reaches for the half pint I just bought, pours it into the pint glass left from her previous drink, (we have been here some time), and opens her mouth to try again, but, finding it all too much for her, knowing I won't like it and that that matters, and, finding her mouth already conveniently open, she fills it with beer; no one can expect her to talk with her mouth full.

But what I really don't believe, what I refuse to believe because I don't like it (she was right) is what she finally summons up courage to say, (was it worth all that courage?)

'Because he's a man, Monica.'

I review the situation in my head. Here I am, sitting in this familiar environment, with the familiar taste of Young's bitter in my mouth, having allowed this same mouth viz: mine to upset the applecart, to grossly overturn the accepted order (words are weapons) and question the assumption, basic to our society, that two women alone in a pub are either waiting for men, or bitching about other women; they are not interested in each other and certainly not (certainly not!) in sex with each other, and this revolting revolution has been achieved by me opening my mouth and, instead of instantly refilling it with beer, employing the few seconds between the last gulp and the yeasty burp (worse with fizzy beer but even Young's Special has its gases) to voice the question:

'Why won't you sleep with me?'

and its counterpart:

'Why do you want to sleep with him?'

Now, don't get me wrong. It wasn't that I felt I had the right to sleep with my best friend. No. But not understanding made me feel angry, which in turn felt very uncomfortable and I had the right to be comfortable.

'Don't get me wrong,' said Rachel, 'my relationship with you, no my friendship, is the most important one in my life, the most important friendship I've ever had.'

I was no nearer understanding, but it was nice she still felt like that. I kept quiet and waited for her to say more. It is always hard for me to keep quiet, especially when I'm nervous. I was nervous.

'I'm sorry, Monica,' said Rachel, 'it's going to be awfully difficult for me to continue this conversation on my own. It gets a bit one-sided. I mean, do you just want to listen in on my flow of consciousness?'

I wanted to laugh. Well, giggle a little. She put it so well, which was why I liked her, which was why I wanted to sleep with her.

'Do you ever imagine sleeping with a woman?' I asked, to change the subject, but it didn't really, did it? Only that was

48

what was on my mind at the time.

'Yes,' she said, 'only I didn't think that was what our relationship was about. In fact, I was surprised you suggested it.'

Surprised? Did that mean she didn't approve? That sleeping was something I did with other women, not her? I wondered was I lowering the tone of our relationship.

'Am I lowering the tone of our relationship?' (I always brought my little problems to Rachel.)

This time she laughed. Well, giggled. So I did too, because that kind of thing is infectious. But I felt it would really be very unfair if even I didn't take my sexuality seriously.

'What on earth are you so afraid of?' I asked, trying to make it sound as neutral as possible.

'I just think it would be very claustrophobic,' she said.

'I'll move out,' I offered.

'You know that isn't what I meant.'

(Why couldn't she see how nice it would be to sleep with someone who knew what she meant?)

'Look, it's no big deal sleeping with someone. I want to sleep with you because I think it would be nice.'

I nearly said 'really nice', but I knew I could never convince her with adverbs. See how cool and calculating I am?

Rachel shook her head. 'I'm going to the bog,' she said, so's I'd know she wasn't walking out on me.

With all that beer I guess one or other of us had to go some time, only it did rather break the flow of our racey dialogue. Like taking time off from watching a glacier. Perhaps I could put it to good use and explain to you out there (and me in here) what it was about me and Rachel that led me to suspect we would end up in bed.

By the end of our first week in college, we had met. I took one look at Rachel and decided, 'This woman is an apolitical hippy'. She listened while I explained how capital punishment should never be taken off the statute book, even if never used, because the state should always have the final say (my days of high Stalinism) and she realised I didn't smoke dope and had probably never heard of Peter Tosh.

We were both dead right.

I went on living on my own in Stamford Hill, thinking I ought to chuck college because it was elitist, while, unbeknownst to me, she and Jock (short for Jocasta, yes I'm afraid so) moved in round the corner. Jock had also noticed her on the first day of term, the only two women nervously sucking cigarettes in the whole room. So Jock and Rae hide in a corner away from the wine and cheese and Jock says:

'I suspect the two of us are going to be inseparable.' Which was a nice thing to say, but it didn't really work in Stamford Hill. They had one room and two dole cheques and they could not get away from each other. Hell, in that flat you couldn't lose sight of one another. So Jock borrowed her mother's dog and they took turns leaving the house and going for a walk.

Which is how come Rae met me in Stoke Newington Cemetery. I used to go there to read. My little pretence at an active social life. I made lists of all the important things I had to do each day and the graveyard always figured prominently after 'wash hair' and 'make bed'. On this particular occasion, the pretence was wearing thin because I hadn't opened my mouth all weekend, and I was wondering just what I'd do if I bought a loaf at Grodzinski's and didn't have the right money, because then I'd have to say something and I wasn't sure I could still do it.

I was lying on a gravestone. Usually I lay on the grass, the mown bit by the tumbled down church because it is softer and warmer, but that day ants kept running across my page, so I'd moved higher up.

Rachel was thinking she shouldn't really have come to the graveyard, because that was where Jock came with the dog and it was just more evidence that she, Rachel, had no mind to call her own; however, now she was here, she didn't see why Jock should keep the place to herself. It was amazing with its solemn flowers hidden behind crumbling tombstones and gothic angels. And hardly anyone around, not like Highgate where she imagined that odd Monica from college went to pay her respects to Marx.

I was thinking what a wowified hippy place the cemetery might have been, only apparently all the yippies hung out in Brighton.

So Rachel and the bounding borzoi (trust Jock's mother to steer clear of anything pronounceable) come round the corner of a grave to find me lying across the stone. I look up to see Rachel obviously in the throes of an ecstatic moment. I am not the total boor my political position would have me seem and I agonise over whether to look down at my book, so she can have her moment in peace, or grunt a quick 'hello' to show I'm not ignoring her. She solves the problem by turning a glowing face towards me and saying:

'It's so fucking far-out.'

Emotion is easy for hippies.

Then she laughs with wide gappy teeth like a Vermeer.

'You remind me of a Vermeer,' I say.

'You look like the Dance of Death,' she says, 'spaced out on that stiffs' slab.'

This time we both laughed and so it continued. Not that we had the same sense of humour, exactly, but we agreed to concentrate on what we had in common, relegating our differences to permanent parenthesis.

Rachel is coming back from the toilet. She is small, but I know the cerulean smock is her. I was there when she bought it and I was there in the Spreadeagle in Camden when the art student leaned over and said:

'Blue, blue is the colour, Peter. Cerulean blue like this peasant's blouse.'

We went around for days sniggering 'blue is the colour' in Maggie Thatcher voices.

I have little time left to remember and I cannot do her the discourtesy of thinking about her in her presence. Of late things have not been going so well. Last week, in an attempt to anticipate her needs, I bought her new light batteries. Hers were flat and she kept forgetting to change them.

'Spose you think I hadn't noticed,' she stormed.

'Why can't you just be pleased?' I asked.

'I think we should have an argument,' she said.

We got out our diaries.

'Wednesday afternoon, Brockwell Park? I'm not really free until then.'

Until Wednesday we were friends. We even managed to go

for a ride together and I lent her my link extractor to tighten her chain. The morning of the argument was sunny and we were unable to decide where to do it, in case it got heavy and people started listening. We had a little practice by the duck pond, but you could tell it hadn't got serious yet.

'I can't bear the way you assume I won't do things and go and do them for me.'

'Crap. I do them for me not for you.'

'Poor little Monica,' said Rachel, 'no ride unless she does all the preparations herself. Look, I am quite capable of getting my shit together, but I have to want to do it.'

'Didn't you want to go for a ride?'

'No. Yes. I don't know why we keep on about that. It just feels like you decide everything, you make it easy for me and I never get a chance to want anything because you've got there first.'

'Oh,' I said bleakly, feeling misunderstood and sorry for myself.

'And you patronise me; showing off your bike to Jock, how it's so much lighter than mine. Dear Rachel, such a sweet child, but not an idea in her head when it comes to bikes.'

'I only meant it as a joke.'

'Sometimes I think you only want me around so you can tell funny stories about me.'

We never reached the top of the hill. By now we were standing in the middle of the path yelling. In a way I was proud we too could have an argument which managed to sound heartfelt. But I was worried. Did I patronise her? Did I treat her like a funny little thing about whom jokes could be made? I was also angry. She appealed to me for help and then resented me giving it. And I was scared. What else had she been storing up and not saying?

'My round?' asked Rachel, hovering, not yet reconciled to the idea of sitting down again.

I shook my head. If she wanted to go she'd have to say so. She blew her non-existent fringe out of her eyes.

'Shall we go then?'

I nodded. It was the first time we'd left a pub before closing time. After the argument it was odd I should choose that night to say what had been in my head for over a year, but I suspected Rachel of turning to this bloke as a way of avoiding the issue. Under the influence of alcohol and the maudlin, drops of unsolicited salt water began to run down my cheeks. Some of them caught on my bottom lip. A voice inside my head suggested Rachel and Monica were going to have to buy separate address books.

'What needless duplication,' I protested loudly (someone had to be on my side, 'we know all the same people and the book just stays next to the phone.'

But when I opened the front door and saw that her bike was no longer stacked against mine but leaning on his, as though they had been out somewhere together, I understood that the anxious voice had been trying to prepare me. Like a mountaineer with vertigo who cannot resist looking down, I paused to gaze at the two bikes nestling against each other in the hallway. Their pedals were intertwined and Rachel's chain was out of gear. She, normally so proud of her upkeep, how could she let herself go like that? His handle bars towered above hers and the whole length of his frame protected her from the world. At a distance stood my bike, only the other side of the carpet, but it could have been worlds away. Its drop handle bars had a droopy, dejected air; its tyres could have done with a good pump. Automatically I wound the off-white tape back round the handle bars, to no more effect than the hundred or so other times I have gone through the same motions.

'Rachel,' I said, before she could burrow off, 'you're lying to me.'

'I'm not,' she said, 'we haven't. I said I'd tell you first.'

'That's what I mean,' I said, 'you knew you had to warn me, but you still say you're surprised.'

'But Monica, you've always known I wasn't a lesbian.'

'It's like you're accusing me of dragging sex into it, but it's always been there. Throbbing away.'

'Stop bullying me. Do you just want me to agree I'm a lousy shit who can't accept responsibility?'

'No,' I thought, 'I want to be able to touch you.'

Silence. We stared at the carpet, realised we were staring at the same patch and looked away.

'I can't stand this,' said Rachel, 'I'm putting the kettle on."

THE FOLD

Janice was appalled and even Helen, who was trying to be on my side because us dykes should stick together, was looking a little nervous and hoping she wasn't going to have to dissociate herself from me.

"No, but I think it's really important that these stereotypes are challenged," said Helen, trying to keep the conversation on an even keel. Janice wasn't having any of it.

"Yes, but to go back to Monica's point; I really can't accept that any woman has the right to question another's sexuality. If I say I'm not into women like that, I expect you to respect it."

"Speaking as a woman 'like that', you have told me, Janice, and I do respect it," I said. "If by 'respect', you mean 'believe'."

"I mean that you should accept that I know what's best for me," Janice said heavily, "not everyone's a lesbian."

"So that's it," I quipped, "I always felt things were not as they could be but I never quite found the words, till they slipped with gentle clarity from your mouth. Like the sun between clouds: not everyone's a lesbian."

"I completely agree that straight women should not assume every lesbian they meet is going to fancy them," said Helen stoutly, still searching for common ground. Which was nice of her, I thought generously, only the rights and assumptions of straight women had precious little to do with me. If they were coward enough to prefer comfort to passion, well. I could have left it there, and we would each have repeated in varying formulae what a pity it was that some lesbians dressed to role; and I would have gone on feeling vaguely uneasy that perhaps I looked too butch; had I no right to be aggressive **because** I was a lesbian; and who

55

dished out the rights anyway, when I felt a sudden surge of fury.

I have been having them more and more often of late: they begin with a sharp stab, forcing me to stare very hard at the floor and bite my nails; then my eyes prickle and I breathe in deeply but slowly, so that no one else will notice; finally, I feel incredibly angry and my whole body is suffused with waves of leaping fury which would hurl me at the throat of the nearest source of displeasure, so that it is all I can do to grip my seat with sweating fingers for the protection of the public, if not my own. There I sit, locked and speechless, till the waves subside, the moment passes, and society regains a daughter.

"Neither," I repeated so there should be no mistaking and Janice would know I meant it, "should they treat us as a bolthole. I'm on nobody's best behaviour and I keep neither my eyes nor my legs leashed."

"Don't mess with Mon," laughed Helen.

"But Monica," said Janice steadily, we have been friends a long time and she didn't want to write me off if there was even a slim chance of salvation, "listen to yourself, if not to me. A woman makes it clear she's not interested, that's enough. Right?"

Helen nodded her fashionable pink feather cut. What else could she do? I was wrong. Everyone knew that. A woman could ruffle your hair and call you treacle, she could borrow your underpants and dispose of your tampax, but as long as she was straight and you were bent, she called the tune. She was a woman with a past, you were a woman without past or future.

"Like you said to me down the Carved Red," chipped in Helen, "it's difficult to know what to do when she's into you and you're not into her. Specially as you're usually not a hundred per cent off, just less enthusiastic."

As true as it was irrelevant.

"Okay," I said, "but what about a woman who ... A woman who makes it quite clear she ... Who says ... " I floundered, but I still had the impression there was something I wanted to say.

"What?" asked Janice, "Mustn't we touch you at all in case it's interpreted as some kind of pass? There's a lot of things women do: walking arm in arm, kissing each other hello, helping with zips, that kind of stuff, which really isn't a turn on. I mean, it doesn't turn me on."

"Stay with it," joked Helen.

"That's not what I mean," I managed. Would I accuse Janice of denial, betrayal or simple falsehood? But this image came into my mind quite unasked. I pushed it away because it wasn't going to help me think clearly, and I was afraid to look at it head on. Like when you ride over a dead cat on the road and you know it's a dead cat, and that that's sad, but you don't want to think about it because it would bring with it a whole morbid train you can do nothing about anyway.

It seems disrespectful to compare Rachel to a dead cat smeared on the road, when she's so astonishingly healthy and her skin shines like fresh olive oil, but she is the image which comes into my mind, and perhaps the dead cat is not her, but my mangled nerves, all tangled together, so that what I feel is radically at odds with what I think. Too late. Rachel, I did try to keep you out, but I didn't want to. Your thick black jumper was there, cuddling me, and you were lying on top of me, holding me close, telling me you didn't want me to move out even if you were sleeping with him, telling me you loved me; and while I wanted to relax and enjoy you hugging me because you didn't want me to go, I couldn't because of what you said about him. I lay there, gripping the cushions, tensing my muscles against you, wanting you to go away and leave me alone, wanting you to stay with me forever. I nearly threw you across the room, smashing your head against the wall, but I didn't. I just lay in your arms. I couldn't even turn the other way round and kiss you, because that's what lesbians do, and you weren't a lesbian. You were comforting a friend who was unhappy.

Then the fury rose up again. Janice and Helen were looking at me, because it was my turn to speak. On the blank wall behind I projected that last scene with Rachel. Reel by reel I showed those two politely patient women what it is like to lie next to another woman, side by side, two bodies touching, naked. What it is like to have her skin brush yours, smooth, soft and warm, her smell as familiar as your own; to have her lean towards you and kiss you lightly, half on the cheek, half in your ear: goodnight. To hate yourself for enjoying the smoothness of her skin, which you are getting on false pretences. You are no longer her old friend, Monica, but a raging beast who would pull her towards you and swallow her, eat her, chew each bone into a thousand splinters. You struggle to get out of bed and sleep somewhere else, but do not want to disturb her with your unwanted feelings. You cannot quite believe they are unwanted. Surely now she will tell you, now she will explain. Yes, she does want you too; yes as deeply as you want her. You are not crazy, or vile, half-man, half-beast. It's just that she can't: her parents won't let her; she has only six months to live; her boyfriend wouldn't like it. Anything. Only not to be crazy. You should have found some way of avoiding this proximity, but you didn't want to avoid it, courted it rather. And she didn't avoid it either, though she knew, she knew.

Janice and Helen were still waiting, women's movement trained, both of them; they would let me speak even if I no longer wanted to.

"What conclusion do you draw from this?" Janice asked gently.

"You been fancying straight women, Mon?" said Helen.

Fancying. How weak, pathetic. I could raze London to the ground with what I felt for Rachel. With one clear, unambiguous 'yes' from her, I could rebuild the whole city with ramps on every street corner, chair lifts in every public building. I could make all the clocks give the same time.

Fancying. And I had broken myself open for them. I had even managed to say Rachel's name out loud.

"But you didn't make love," Janice was saying reasonably, "I mean, it wasn't a sexual relationship, was it?"

"Go on," scoffed Helen, "sleeping naked does have cultural implications."

I didn't think I could bear to have them discuss me and Rachel in bed. I listened to Janice telling me it wasn't sexual. It was the same voice that told me I shouldn't have short hair because it only fed the stereotype, that lesbians were okay as long as they didn't draw any conclusions, that anger [or any other excess emotion] was the province of therapy and best deposited there.

"It wasn't sexual, was it?" I repeated. "Think you own the

58

world, you do. The whole bloody world. Think you can decide what part equals sex, what part is friendship and what's left over gets wrapped up as sisterhood. Well, sisterhood's toothpaste, as far as I'm concerned. Whitewash to hide the cracks."

Better than staring at the floor or biting my nails.

"Sleeping naked has cultural implications," I continued. "Good grief, you buy that do you, Helen? That all Angie means to you? Simply prefer women because you like the shape of our bodies."

"No," said Helen, uneasy at my vehemence, reluctant to take sides, "of course not. But, does it have to be so polarised?"

"You make me feel like a naughty child, encouraging me to return to the fold."

Here at last was something Helen could recognise.

"If by 'fold' you mean solidarity, then I do think you could try to see Janice's point of view."

"A fold," I said nastily, "is an enclosure for sheep. You can't very well miss Janice's point of view. She has it pasted up on every tube station."

"That's not fair," Helen protested, "now you know that, Monica."

"Well perhaps it's time we stopped being fair," I said, "and recognised our moral superiority." Whether Rachel ever admitted it, she had wanted me. She was the coward, the beast; it was she who had got me on false pretences.

BEDROCK PASSION

". . . my lovers will be women
for whom loving women
is already a clear and
bedrock passion
. . .
not an experience
on the basis of which
they will make a decision
about their sexuality
or politics
or both".
Sheila Shulman.

Perhaps you should pause now and look up the rest of the poem. It's on page 215 of *One Foot On The Mountain*. Or perhaps Ai should type it out and put it above her bed next to the Sheba poster – the one that suggests it's easy really, if only we were just a touch more open.

On Sunday, during a conference on Women Writers, which most seemed to interpret as 'women note-takers', this being the chief activity of the audience, while the famous few talked to them about success, Ai, whose mind was not used to the confines of vicarious glory, decided momentously that she wanted to live with other lesbians because women weren't good enough. This led to the problem of how to tell her flat mate; whether the women in Stockwell would have her, and whether they were the sort of lesbians she wanted to share a house with. So, when at college the next day, Jo, a resolute non-lesbian, said she would like to go for a drink with her one night, Ai had time only to see it as a petty annoyance which would have to be got through in the interests of the warm working relationship she enjoyed with her female colleagues, before releasing her brain for more pressing matters.

"Groan," she intimated to Lee, "I wish there was something I could take her to. The thought of listening for a whole evening while she tells me how she and John aren't allowed to sleep together at home . . ."

But in the end she was too busy booking tickets for Sisterhood of Spit, explaining things to her flat mate, and sussing out the women in Stockwell, to fix up any form of entertainment for Jo on Thursday night. Jo arrived for dinner and they went down the pub.

"Same as usual?" said Jo, "Pint of bitter?"

"Yes," said Ai, mildly surprised; she wondered what it was Jo drank.

"This is where you usually meet Sarah and the others," said Jo, looking round with interest.

"Yes," said Ai, she hadn't realised she'd mentioned them to Jo.

"Tell me about this Writers' Group," Jo asked.

"Well," said Ai, not wanting to deliver anything important into her hands, "there's not much to say, really, we're lesbians and . . .

"I thought you were," said Jo with the look of someone who's guessed right.

"Then why didn't you make it easier for me?"

"Well, I mean, it would have been embarrassing if I was wrong."

"Interesting you should say that."

"Why do you think that is?"

"You mean why do I think you find lesbians embarrassing?"

"No, why do you think you're a lesbian?"

Nice to have a mentor, Ai thought, but why pick me?

Ai shrugged, with only the slightest raise of an eyebrow, unwilling to give away even her contempt.

"What did you make of my flat mate?" she asked, and

there followed a comfortable, impersonal discussion on the politics of apartheid and whether white South Africans were justified in going back. Ai even found time to play over the women in Stockwell, and by the time the argument was over, (Jo won hands down, unilateral boycott was the only solution), Ai had decided she probably would like to move in there.

"I hope Laura hasn't gone to bed yet."

"?"

"The spare mattress is in her room."

"Oh, I wouldn't want to put you to the bother."

"Really? It's not worth my making up another bed?"

"No, honestly Ai, I'd rather sleep with you."

"Okey doke, saves the sheets."

If she washed them by hand they'd freeze on the line in this weather.

Ai got into bed and shivered. Not the best time to move house. She wished she could find a permanent home for her books. She kept promising them a place of safety, but every six months they were uprooted and lugged off some place else. Jo got in beside her. For a while their teeth chattered in unison. Jo turned towards Ai and giggled. She rubbed Ai's arms to warm her. It is difficult to keep aloof from someone who is holding you. Ai wanted someone to hold her. Hold her very close and not let go. Not want to let go. Ever. Jo rubbed her arms and shoulders, stroked her, hugged her. Ai wanted someone to touch her body and she didn't think she could afford to be fussy.

"I don't feel sexually excited," said Jo, after a while. "I just thought I should tell you that."

"Oh, quite right," said Ai, struggling to regulate her breathing. "For God's sake let's be honest, if we can't be anything else."

"You are, though, aren't you?" said Jo, "I can tell."

"Don't you ever find honesty a bit of a luxury?"

"Well, you see, I just didn't imagine it quite like this."

"Oh, I am sorry."

"I did talk it over with John, and he said I should go ahead and ask you out, but we didn't really discuss what it would be like."

"What a pity."

"Do you mind me telling John about you?"

"Well, now you come to mention it . . ."

"Yes, I anticipated this."

"Did you, dear?"

"Mmmm, well, I wanted to think about what was going to happen."

"You know," said Ai, trying to say something near to what she was thinking, "I'm going to find it difficult being in college with you tomorrow and not able to touch you."

"Yes, I thought it would be better if we missed sociology."

"What a good idea."

Then Jo told Ai how awful it was at home. How she and her sister drifted apart when they used to be so close, closer ever than friends. After her year in France, Jo no longer thought in Irish, so when she spoke to her sister, Kath said she sounded like a foreigner.

"Honestly, Ai, we used to share everything when we were at school. My mother had a breakdown and when we visited her in hospital, she thought we were her sisters. She kept calling for us, even though we were there. It was terrible. Oh my poor mam."

Despite everything, Ai was touched and interrupted herself musing on what language Jo dreamed in, French, English or Gaelic, to look at Jo's face from her side of the moonlight.

"Poor mouse."

"I've never told anyone about it save John."

Ai was moved by Jo's loneliness, but when she continued with the tale of her school friend, Ellen, it sounded like a statutory set piece.

"We were in bed together one night, you know, sharing a mattress."

"I know," said Ai.

"And she said she felt physically attracted to me."

"And you said you were flattered, but you just weren't into women, at least not in that way."

"Pretty much. Why, what do you think about it? You sound critical."

"I was thinking poor Ellen."

"What's the time?" said Jo. She asked this at regular intervals, as though it was necessary to talk all night for passion to have taken place.

In the morning Jo explained to Ai that though she was fond of her, as far as she knew her, her main commitment was to John, who was not only her boyfriend, but her best friend.

"How neat," said Ai.

"Now, if you want to see me during the holidays, this is where I'll be."

Ai looked at the piece of paper wih the address in Hull, the address in Ireland and the various dates.

It took them two hours to get to college because of the snow. At Victoria Station there were two police officers gazing intently at the flakes as they settled unperturbed on the railway track.

"Look, Jo," said Ai, "they'll have to make a report."

"Severe breach of the peace by a bunch of snowflakes," Jo added, "they'll have to send for reinforcements."

The two women laughed, and as the train took them off to Richmond, they stared out at the whiteness and the station lamps which seemed to have been painted in at the last minute, they shone out so yellow and artificial against the real colour of the snow. The electric wires were all black save one, which was purple. Ai hadn't noticed that before. She showed it to Jo so as not to talk about anything else.

"I wish I had my camera," said Jo.

"But Jo, you were so contemptuous yesterday of the students in college taking photos in the snow. You were sure they'd be overexposed."

"You remember too much," said Jo, looking pleased.

Ai wondered about it. Perhaps she had paid more attention than she thought.

"How do you feel now?" Jo asked.

"Well, I suppose it does change my relationship to college."

"To college!"

But Ai refused to alter what she'd said.

That weekend she felt furious. Furious to find Jo's tooth brush and flannel in a little plastic bag by the mirror, furious not to see her till Tuesday, furious to be experimented on and found wanting, furious to be in such a state that she would accept sex on those terms.

On Tuesday she gave Jo a neatly typed copy of the poem

by Sheila Shulman, just as she was going off to see a supervisor.

"I'd like you to read this," Ai said, "I think it's relevant."

The next time she saw Jo was down the pub at lunchtime with the others. Jo sat opposite her on a stool, hunched up in her coat, though everyone else had taken theirs off. Ai wanted to touch her and ask was it alright. Looking at Jo, she didn't feel angry anymore. There was a conversation about the ineptitude of one of the lecturers; Ai rolled off the adjectives, Jo said nothing.

Ai had felt so relieved to find the poem in the anthology, to know that it would be there when she looked, that she wasn't on her own and didn't have to rethink the wheel, as Lee put it. That was why literature was important, validating, supportive, but she shouldn't have thrust them at Jo like an ultimatum.

"I'm going back to college," Ai said, "what about you, Jo?"

"I'm off home."

But in the library Ai turned and Jo was there, eyes wide. She threw her arms round Ai and said,

"I have to talk to you."

So they talked and walked by the river, and Ai forgave Jo for experimenting, and admitted Jo could not be the cause of all her misery, and Jo said she was sorry, but she had no one else to talk to, because there were some things you couldn't say to John. And Jo talked about her doubts, her fears and her inadequacy and Ai talked a bit about hers. On Richmond Bridge, they kissed each other, which, Ai reflected, was a brave thing for Jo to do, and left it at that.

Except that on Friday Ai got very drunk at the benefit for Sisterhood of Spit, arrived on her own, talked to an awful lot of women at the rate of three minutes each.

"About as long as they can stick me," she thought. Lee even turned and walked away but Ai didn't feel she could blame her.

In the end she gave in to it and cried, and the next day she cycled to Stockwell.

LITTLE MOMENTS OF ETERNITY

One

Stella watched as Louisa turned and swam back. She wore a bathing cap the same pastelgreen as her costume. Up and down. Up and down. Stella had given up counting lengths. With her regular breast-stroke and slightly screw kick, her face held just above water-level, expressionless for fear of wrinkles, Louisa could have been paid by the hour. Like gently trickling water, she provided just enough lazy activity for the hotel guests to feel justified in dozing off in the sun.

The children had gone with Robert to look round the hot white city and eat strange-coloured sweets in the shade. Eager and penitent as a Sunday father, he would charge them around relentlessly, until they grew tired and bored him, to be delivered to their mother: two over-excited animals for her to calm down and put to bed.

Louisa scarcely touched the side as she glided round to go back again. Her body, now blurred in outline by the water, on land was firm and stream-lined. It held no secrets. Not that Stella, acquainted since the night before with every soft brown mole, every broken vein, knew it so well that it held no secrets for her. Simply, it held no secrets. There were no broken veins and the soft brown mole, if ever soft brown mole there had been, had long been electrolysed away. Last night Stella had touched her. Just. But it had been a near thing, and Louisa resented it. Stella could not make love without wanting the whole world.

The sun had very nearly dried up the path of high-arched footprints that led from the pool to Stella's table.

"We have all afternoon," Louisa had said, shielding her eyes from the sun and looking directly into Stella's. Provocative was within the rules. She dripped fat puddles onto the hot concrete and her chest heaved faintly with exertion. Stella was not immune to it, but lust is never self-contained. It seemed somehow ignoble to think of Louisa's body, while gazing into her eyes, yet she could not imagine touching any part of it without her knickers feeling damp and uncomfortable.

"They'll squabble in the back of the car," she replied, "and Robert will tell them if they don't shut up he'll dump them off . . ."

"And they won't shut up," Louisa continued . . .

"So he'll have to dump them off," they both finished together, laughing.

Stella shook her head. "I'm tired of being grateful for the little bottle someone else gave me as a favour." She wondered if Louisa understood.

Louisa understood alright, but she was not making any more decisions because someone else wanted her to. And she retraced her steps to the pool before the first set of prints had time to dry.

Two

A woman goes to pick up a child from playgroup. The woman is tired. The child is not tired and does not want to go home yet. The woman had not been thinking about the child. She seemed to think she was posting a letter; something she had said she would do, not a thing to be worked at or enjoyed. At first, as all the other children were leaving and there was a general movement up the path, the child came, if not willingly, at least dispassionately. But as they walked along the street, the child lagged further and further behind. Inside it would be dark and there was so much to do out here: bright flowers fallen on the road, workmen on their tea-break, a big pile of sand to walk on, sift and pat. The child sat down on the sand.

"I don't want to go home."

The woman turned round and saw her for the first time since spotting her orange T shirt among the others. The woman was not in a hurry either, but she did not like to lose control. How long would the child scream if she simply picked her up and carried her? Did they have to have a row? She did not want the child to dislike her.

The child on the sand; the woman watching, anxious, ineffectual. It was the child who resolved the problem. An idea glimmered in her mind; the woman had none.

"You get my bucket and we spill the sand in, okay?"

The woman smiled. The child nodded encouragement.

"Okay," said the woman with sudden enthusiasm for the hot day, the soft sand and the smiling child. "Come on and we'll get it together. We can take it into the garden and I'll fill up the watering can."

The child jumped to her feet and they ran together into the house.

A woman and a child tickle each other with blades of grass. You have to do it right, soft enough and in the right place: behind the ears, across the neck and down the middle of the backbone. The child's back is brown with tiny black hairs along the spine; she is wearing only white knickers.

The woman's name is Stella, but who is the child? Brenda's daughter? Louisa's daughter? She picks up a dandelion, losing half the fluff as she tugs;

"What time is it, Stella?"

Dandelions. London. It must be Brenda's daughter. Soon she will come home and thank Stella for having Stevie, and Stella will wish she had simply posted a letter.

Three

Stella had taken her place in the queue to check-in at Heathrow. She had tried to explain to Brenda that she could go now because she had something to leave, but the words were circular. She was going because recently, when walking back from the pub, she had seen a snake slither across the pavement in front of her. She had been frightened, though she was not afraid of snakes. She was going because when the sun was bright it made her want to walk barefoot and you couldn't do that here. And because she hadn't watched Twizzle as a little girl; because she could still walk across Waterloo Bridge and feel excited just to be there. Well, she supposed all lesbians were foreigners; though it might sound exotic to be different, it is hard to have no country, and even the community we make, we call a 'ghetto', in case our need for it shows through. But there was more. There was the feeling of crashing tower blocks and clinging to the railings because she did not know where she was. After years of people saying 'gosh' and envying her cultural diversity, she had hoped, overcoming a certain distanced cynicism, to find women who could see it might have its drawbacks. Distance was a hard layer to lose — too hard, she reflected, as she sought escape in a place where she couldn't possibly fit.

In front of her in the queue was a very clean American family. Little girl was hugging a doll which exactly resembled herself; little boy wore a small suit and a haircut that showed his ears; daddy was smoothly but unobtrusively tanned. Mommy sat on a bench waiting for Robert to finish with the luggage. She waited graciously and with great concentration: she would be good at keeping calm in a crisis, but Robert took care of everything.

Stella wondered did she have the maid put peppermint in the final rinse?

"Where you people from?" asked the Young American behind her with the tall openness of one who comes from somewhere himself.

"Washington," said Robert, totally frank, giving nothing away.

"Well," thought Stella, it was better than listening to herself.

On her bench Louisa smiled vaguely. Her husband's small tragedy was that he had nothing to give away.

Did Americans genuinely like each other? Stella could think of nothing more sordid than claiming nationality as a bond, when the honest handshakes marked a comradeship nothing disputed.

"I'm afraid you're overweight, sir," the stewardess was saying to Robert, as she heaved the eighth matching leather suitcase onto the scales.

"Aw, he's just a little paunchy," said the Jock, failing to follow this through with a friendly dig in the belly only because the cases were in the way. He pointed to Stella.

"Why, sir, this good lady has only one itsy little bag. I'm sure she wouldn mind you takin her extra kilos."

Stella showed no sign of surprise that Americans, having so much to begin with, should claim still more because of it.

Their boarding passes now doomed them to sit together. Stella settled down with *Cactus*, a charmed circle 5,000 feet up. Louisa, having smiled her way out of her husband's conversation, sipped her sherry and looked blank. Stella turned a page. Disturbed. Her preoccupations were such that everything her mind touched became metabolised into the one thought. In the book Ann and Dee were breaking out of the 'ghetto', just as she had been searching for it. And she'd found it: something to do with where you spent Christmas.

"An what do you do, little lady? Or are you married to the pilot?" said Jock.

"I'm going to teach English at the Christian Mission in Gaya," said Stella, seeking protection in the Catholic Church.

"Why I'd got you taped as a millionaire heiress."

Robert caught his wife's eye and winked.

"These two oddballs deserve each other."

He didn't mind women being ugly, but he would not forgive them for not trying. He could imagine his wife taking pity on her and offering her a job as a nanny. She had the accent and Lord knows, she was in no danger from him.

Stella was thinking about Brenda.

"Well," she had said, as they celebrated the last of Stella's exams, "now you can be somebody's English teacher."

"Somebody in India," said Stella, unaccustomed as she was to dropping bombshells, only Brenda sounded like she was welcoming her into the workforce.

"Oh Stella, I'll be lonesome for you," Brenda replied lightly. Had Stella looked to Brenda for the ultimate reason to go?

Don't go, Stella, I love you.

Don't go, Stella, I need you.

Don't go, Stella, I'll drop Kathryn for you.

When they were in bed and Stella was in tears: demanding but not explicit, Brenda relented.

"Whatever did you expect? Faced with your ultimatum."

Stella left no room to negotiate; she made neatly packaged statements of intent. She could not ask for more because the rest of Brenda's time was for Kathryn.

Brenda would say this wasn't true; that her arrangement with Kathryn, though of long standing, could alter; and anyway, what did Stella want?

Still Stella would not say what she wanted, and Brenda would have to be getting back – to Kathryn, to her daughter, to herself.

"I had no more say in it than if you'd been a man."

"A man? Jesus fuck."

"Well, you're behaving like a runaway child who wants her reasons guessed and answered."

"I was born in 55. I have no right to talk till 1990?"

"It bothers you that much to be younger than me?"

"It obviously bothers you."

"When Helen was having a Sixties party you asked what kind of music they played then. The Sixties! Stella, come off it."

"Yeah, that was stupid."

"It was crass."

"Well, I make some point or other and 5 minutes later you start up with 'I think what Stella's really trying to say . . .' "

Brenda would quite like to have gone to sleep. Some people had jobs to go to.

"Why, Stella, I do believe you're angry."

"It's no good staying calm with you lot. You don't listen

till someone piles on the invective."

"Who's 'you lot', Stella?"

"All of you. You and Kathryn and Helen and the others in the collective. You are. You do. You all talk the same, about 'doing numbers' and 'wittering on' and things being 'deeply something or other'."

Stella stared at the American's hand on his wife's knee. She could have done with one of 'that lot' now. The plane began its descent towards Delhi. What would happen in Calcutta? There were three days before she was expected at the school. Was it worth offering to look after the kids? Younger, she might have sailed through it, blithely naive of the dangers, but she was not going to spend another night alone in a foreign hotel with men banging on the door, determined that if she wasn't that kind of girl already, she was going to be. And three days was too long to spend thinking: if you didn't like the heat, you opened a window, you didn't set up house in a fridge.

"Stop threatening and go," Brenda had said finally.

She'd said a lot of other things in between. "You can't have it all, so you don't want any. You want a shadow not a lover."

"Do you know, there are people here living on the pavements?" said Robert, "Building little lean-to shelters; mothers suckling their young right out in the open."

"One thing they can't clear up for the tourists," said Louisa.

"She should worry," thought Stella, "she gets her cocktails at the Flying Club either way."

"They have their pride," said the Jock, "wouldn't trade their freedom for one of our apartment blocks."

Stella thought of her refusal to get a job that paid because she'd have to wear tights and be circumspect. There was no comparison. Louisa thought of leaving her husband, wearing flat shoes or neglecting to watch her weight. What freedom?

73

She couldn't even take the kids.

An electric bus drove them to the transit lounge. There were jokes about germs and curry powder. Stella felt ashamed to speak English, yet she was recolonising this country with her language.

"You're answering an ad their government put out and besides," Brenda twinkled at her breadth of general knowledge, "in the fifties there were riots when they tried to replace English with Hindi. English was colonial, but Hindi meant Indian oppression."

Before they entered the terminal, they were frisked. Quick and efficient, but embarrassing to be patted like that by strangers, to have sex thrust into one's head in such an incongruous way.

"Imagine Customs doing this at JFK," said Jock, "or Heathrow," he added, for international perspective.

"They do," said Stella, bitterly, avoiding more personal sentiment, "far worse. Asian women are subjected to crackpot virginity tests, by men who aren't even doctors. One woman gave birth in a Detention Centre and they wouldn't take her to hospital because they didn't want it born on British soil."

"Still suffering from moments of omnipotence?" Brenda would jibe. Her little catchphrase.

One night Stella's feelings of passionate lust had led her to turn to Brenda and say,

"I do love you, you know."

And Brenda had laughed gently and said,

"Your little moment of eternity."

"I'm sure it's the same in the States," said Louisa, "only one hasn't heard about it." And she sat down on another bench and practised waiting some more. From the zip pocket of her hand luggage she pulled a cardboard cut-out doll and a book of steam trains.

"Here you are, Karen, now what colour will you do Puffing Billy?"

"Blue," said Karen, "no red, no green," snatching the pens so her brother couldn't get them.

Louisa was so good at it, the way she extracted the scissors as soon as Bobby had finished with the doll.

"This is disgraceful," Robert was saying, with all the dignity of the American Ambassador he was not, "they say we'll be stuck here three hours. How about a ride into town?"

"What a good idea," said Louisa evenly, "but I think I'll rest a while in the air-con."

Armed with official clearance, the men set off to explore. Louisa took herself to the bathroom.

"I'm afraid it's not even up to French standards."

Were all Americans obsessed with plumbing?

"My husband says in their homes they have bowls of water not paper. Don't ask me what they do with them."

Would she hit the ceiling or Louisa first? Was sisterhood really supposed to find space for this rich racist bitch?

"India," she began determinedly, "is a Third World country. A poor country. Poverty? Yes? You've heard of it, maybe. Something to do with the urchin look, only all year round. There are people here starving to death. You know hunger? When you've eaten your full quota of Limmits and have no calories left. Paper is expensive: you have to chop down trees, which is no good for the water supply. People wipe their bums with their hands here. Okay? That solve the mystery? It's cleaner that way and it's better for them and what's more, I imagine it feels good."

Louisa took her time. The children were asleep, arms and legs sprawled all over the place. She leaned over and straightened them before turning to Stella. "Better for them? Better than what? Better for Indians or would it be better for us too? India is very lucky to have you as its spokesman. Perhaps you'd like to do a cultural survey of the States sometime. But tell me, is your morbid interest in poverty the product of a sterile homelife or do you expect constant allowance for your extreme youth?"

75

Four

In a family suite on the fifteenth floor of the Ridgeway Hotel, Calcutta, Stella and Louisa turned aside and reached simultaneously for their glasses.

"I can't get over this room service number," said Stella, "pink gin at three am."

"I can't get over this woman in my bed," said Louisa and for a while she didn't try.

Stella ran her hand along Louisa's side:

"After what you said in Delhi . . ."

"But you were such a self-righteous brat. You stormed off to the bathroom like you were going to liberate the masses."

"My half-baked attempt at solidarity. I even put some money in the saucer."

"If I hadn't asked for help with the kids . . ."

"If we hadn't been bathing them together . . ."

"No, it wasn't like that."

"?"

"I planned it, Stella. 'Reds in the bed', you know what they say. Besides, I was lonely."

"Life with Robert seems to allow plenty of planning time."

"Will you stay, then? Robert's very honourable about wages."

It was tempting. The taste of wealth was like half a chocolate eclair.

"Just when I thought I was earning my percentage of the whiskey money, you offer me the little bottle. Will I drink it or sell it?"

"Is it the gin or my intoxicating beauty?"

Stella laughed. "Let me tell you what happened after I went to the toilet. I was just drying my hands, when the attendant came towards me, a ten dollar bill in her hands."

"You buy me duty-free whiskey?"

At first I just stared at her, the note was so old it was soft. I didn't understand what she was asking. I wanted to tell her to save the money, buy a gun and shoot the bastards.

"Who were you?" asked Louisa.

76

"The avenging angel."

"But what the woman wanted was a bottle of whiskey."

"I took the money. It felt like a damp tissue. I crumpled it in my hand and turned to go."

"You said nothing to the woman?"

"I wanted to think of the danger we were in."

"A white woman in an international transit lounge. You were in no danger."

"There was a state of emergency. The woman could have been planted."

"Planted to catch tourists guilty of liberal conscience?"

"It's the right money," said the assistant, eyes on the door.

I went straight to the counter. There was a long queue; I could have been buying a tube ticket.

"The flight was from London, you were British. There was no reason to be carrying American currency."

"I would have said I'd got it from you."

"You trusted me even then?"

"She trusted me first."

My palms began to sweat, I shredded the Kleenex in my pocket.

"Yes, madam, and for you? Perfume, Eau de Cologne?"

"I stared at the man. I didn't see him. I felt the bits of paper in my hand."

"You thought it was the dollar bill?"

"I thought it was the bank-note."

"But you'd torn the paper hanky in your fear."

"In my rage."

"You were angry because you'd been asked to buy whiskey, because the woman didn't ask for very much."

"She wanted a bottle of whiskey."

"A bottle of Haig, please."

"You pay Sterling?"

"No. American dollars."

"Do you want your change in rupees?"

"Change?"

I very nearly said that. I nearly asked what change.

"She said it was the right money."

"The rate of exchange must have altered."

"She can't have known the price had gone down."

"No," I said. "Not rupees. I'll have one of those little bottles as well."

"She would make more of a profit . . ."

"Didn't you think she would drink it?"

"It wasn't for me to decide."

"You put the bottles in your bag. They clinked together as you walked, as if you were going to a party."

"I felt like the conveyor of stolen goods."

"I was frightened. I had to get away."

"You wondered was the cashier in it too. You could not remember how he looked at you."

"I was frightened, I had to get away."

"You wondered what part the black market played in the Indian economy."

"It would not be seriously threatened by two bottles of contraband."

"Thinking it might look suspicious to return right away to the Ladies, you examined the glass display case with its silk scarves, its ivory, its saris."

"I rank the silk through my fingers but they shook like a typewriter table."

"Dread was worse than apprehension."

"When I opened the door of the toilet . . ."

"The woman was waiting impatiently . . ."

"I took out the big bottle first . . ."

"You wondered how to explain . . ."

"That whiskey was harder currency than rupees . . ."

"And there was no change."

"Suddenly the door opened . . ."

"And two men walked into the room."

"Their voices were high and urgent . . ."

"They picked up the bottle of whiskey."

"And slipped off as quick as they came."

"I stared at the woman in silence, angry that . . ."

"You were angry that what you thought was an affair between women was really controlled by men."

So anyway, I waited till things quietened down again and some woman came in to get something.

"That was me," whispered Louisa, "I'd left my eye-lash curlers by the faucet." And she kissed Stella on the ear.

Stella snorted. "I must have washed my hands five times in there. Finally I took out the second bottle."

"Was she pleased, the Indian woman?"

"I couldn't tell."

"But the men might have found out and beaten her."

"Oh, no she sold it and saved up to buy a gun."

"I'm glad it ends happily, though I wish she got all the profits."

"She didn't own the original capital."

"Women never do."

Five

Stella took one last look at the green mosaic of the pool, built in the shape of a dolphin; the reflected ripples dappling the white wall opposite; the tower of balconies decked with bath towels which closed off the pool from the street. The last of the damp footprints had now disappeared.

PAMELUMP

When Pamela's mum heard me calling her daughter 'Pamelump', she went all grey and quiet. Not grown-up type serious, like when they catch you telling a dirty joke, or saying a rude word, but really grey, like after someone's been sick. I thought she was going to burst into tears, if she didn't hit me first. Pamelump noticed everything: her mum going grey, me being scared I'd get the belt, then scared I'd hurt her mother. Pamelump always noticed. She had to. We went right on playing though. First, because it wasn't fair to strain Pamelump's memory by making her keep too much for too long. Seeing as she couldn't just note things down like I could. Second, because you have to. They're always turning grey, or green, or shakey, and you have to go on as though you hadn't noticed. How they feel is their problem and you have to keep it that way. All they want is to pass it on to you.

Actually, the rules were more complicated than that because, whatever you do, and however much you go on playing, they have said it, and you have heard it. They were Pamelump's rules. She said sometimes it was much worse when everyone pretended, because then she couldn't be offended, or angry, or anything.

When we were younger and the driver took us into town, I wheeled Pamelump places to look at windows and shops or to play with water. I had to steer her over the smoothest ground, and make sure to check beforehand that her tyres were full but not hard, otherwise she got jolted down in the chair and couldn't see anything but sky. All the kids would crowd round.

"Why's she in a chair? She's older than my boetje and he walks by himself."

"Can I push? My mum lets me push our baby."

"Where's your legs? Why've you got no legs?"

"Never grew in my mum's tummy." Her most generous explanation.

"Forgot to bring them, didn't I?" When she was feeling sarky.

"Same place as my arms." That's when she was angry and wanted to shock. It's such a small town, Luanshya; most of the kids knew her. But there were always some. A cousin from Ndola or a new family fresh out from Scotland. They said that no one had warned them, but I think some kids are naturally spiteful. Then they'd want to see what she looked like under the shawl, even the ones who'd looked before. They wanted to see how a shoulder goes when it doesn't have an arm on it. I know what they wanted because I was like that when my mum first told me. Now that I've washed her and dressed her, shaken her with fury and patted her so often, I know what she looks like. Just exactly the way you would expect a girl to look who doesn't have arms or legs. Where you or me go on, she stops. That's all.

Her mother had the African dressmaker cut Pamelump trousers with long legs, long-sleeved shirts, to pretend she might have arms and legs to fill them. But Pamelump complained she couldn't use her stumps with all that cloth flapping around. If people didn't like the look of her, they could look elsewhere. Well, the kids looked and the grown ups looked away. I couldn't tell which hurt Pamelump worse. She made excuses why we couldn't go places: the shops had too many steps, it was too hot to sit under a shawl. Then we stopped going anywhere except the bush and the farm where we wouldn't meet anyone who didn't belong to Pamelump.

Pamelump didn't really need to go anywhere. Her teachers came to her and she sent things away to England for correcting. Mostly her books returned marked 'excellent'. Pamelump was more proud of that than anything because the English teachers didn't know about her and couldn't have been marking her up. She worked out everything in her head then typed it with her chin, or checked it on her computer, though she had to programme the computer. Her mother asked if I'd like to have my lessons with Pamelump, too. I would've, very much, even though Pamelump was a year older and much quicker. But my mum said, "I do draw the line at that. I'm afraid I really do draw the line at that. We said you could befriend her, and with your father away the money comes in handy, Lord knows, but really! If you spend any more time with that poor little lump, you'll forget what normal is."

Pamelump was my best friend, but I did have other friends. Girls at school I could run, skip and play British bulldog with, so I wasn't in any danger. Besides, with the radio and the papers, and the way people acted, Pamelump knew what normal was and she wasn't even it.

"My mum says it's really kind of you to go and sit with that poor little Pamela."

"My mum says she'll die soon and that's a kindness to all. They don't live past puberty."

"What's puberty?"

Pamelump used to ask me what my friends said. She already knew about puberty. She was watching out for it. And she knew all my friends' names. Her mother invited them to her birthday parties and some of them would come, on their best behaviour. But they could really only play British bulldog and skipping, so they weren't much fun for Pamelump.

"We going on the trampolines, Wendy, you coming with?"

"Ner. Pamelump's driver's coming for me."

"You play there every arvo. They should get a black to sit with her." I didn't like having to tell Pamelump what the other girls said. I didn't like the way she called them 'your friends', as though I agreed with them. It wasn't as though she didn't know. I already said about her noticing everything.

"You only come because my mother pays you. You're just like all the other shoppers."

'Shoppers' is what she called people paid for friendship. She was like that about the servants too. They were always kind to her, but she said it was because they were Africans and had no choice. She wanted them to love her just because. I said it was true we were poor, and my mum needed the money with my dad away, but I came to see her because she was my friend. She ignored that and asked: "Where's your dad, then?" "Away." "Away where?" "He'll be home soon." "I know where your dad is." "Where is he, then?" "He's in prison." "No he's not." "He is." "How do you know anyway?" "Cos I read the papers not Teddy Bear Annual." I didn't know what to say. "He never did it. He's an innocent man." "Never did what?" "What they say." Pamelump looked at me. "He sold tickets on the trains. But sometimes he didn't give any ticket. He kept the money instead." "No he never. My mum says he never. And they're going to prove it and then they'll have to let him out and apologise in front of everyone." Pamelump sneered at me, "So my only friend is a liar and her father's a thief." If it would of been anyone else, I would of slapped her. Instead I sneered right back, "And my only friend has no arms, no legs and no brain." "Your dad's cape coloured." "And your mum lets her daughter play with one cos no one else would do it." "See, see!" yelled Pamelump, "I was right all along. You only come cos you're paid to. You shopper. Shopper. Shopper. Tickey hopper." "I won't be your friend any more." "Then what will your mum do? Have to get a job instead of sending you out." "She's got a job." And then I remembered and started to cry and couldn't stop. Usually Pamelump's good about crying, but after what she said I didn't want to be anywhere near her anymore. I ran out into the bush and hid in the mealies.

"So you're a coward as well as a liar," Pamelump stormed at me from her chair. I should have heard it bumping over the ground. "You can just run off and leave me."

"And you can get Benjamin to wheel you after." Benjamin turned away to examine the mealies. We got used to having our rows in front of people.

"Well," said Pamelump as if she was beginning to be nice again, "what are you so upset about?"

"My mum," I told her, "she fainted at work. They sent her home. Now she's scared they won't take her back cos of my dad. They keep telling her to stay home and rest and it must be a very difficult time for her."

"Why did she faint?"

"Cos she didn't eat anything. I never noticed. She always said she ate breakfast after me and my brothers went to school. But it wasn't true. She didn't eat anything."

"Why though?" asked Pamelump, "Why didn't she eat?

Was it because she was upset?"

"No! There wasn't anything to eat. She gave it all to us."

"It's alright, Wendy. It's not your fault. You just thought you were being good and eating your breakfast not to worry your mother."

"Yes," I sniffed, "I didn't know."

"And my mum will give your mum some money. Till your dad gets out."

"No," I said, "my mum wouldn't take it."

Pamelump looked at me. A funny little look, like making a child confess she's fibbing.

"No, honestly. She hates taking your mum's money."

"Then my mum must ring up the shop where she works and tell them they can't sack her."

"You can't tell your mum anything," I said, "my mum says the fewer know the better."

"Mum's alright about most things," said Pamelump. "It's only me she's funny with."

I don't know what Pamelump told her mother, but they let my mum go back to work and she had her meals in the canteen like salaried staff. After they'd eaten. All alone in the great big kitchen.

Pamelump did all sorts of things no one else did. I don't just mean thinking up strings to pull with her teeth, levers she could press with her tongue, but the games we played. She stored it in her memory to save herself the trouble of moving things around. She would think through whole crossword puzzles or chess games just gazing at the empty pattern, and she was always right the times she asked me to write it down for her. That's how she played our games, but she made up no-arms-no-legs-games that were much more exciting. She said if you thought who got paid how much for doing what, it was obvious that all work consisted of was moving things around in the world. The further you were from the actual moving, the more you got paid. So we played moving games, where you touch nothing and remember everything.

"I give up, Pamelump, I don't know how Vincenza The Invincible is going to escape Brute Beit. You've got her hanging upside down on a meat hook, and it's Cecil Rhodes Birthday so even if she gets away, no one will be around to give her tickey for a phone call."

That's when Pamela's mother turned grey.

"Wendy, dear, I'm afraid it's time for you to go now. I'll drive you. No need to wait for Benjamin."

But you remember it all, don't you, Pamelump? Because it's you I'm talking to. There isn't anyone else. There simply isn't. I wonder if you knew what it would be like afterwards? I tell the story to myself often, to keep it alive, and it sounds strange now. Written down. I have never spoken of it to anyone. Never. To anyone. Do you know what that means? I try to keep it in order, in time at least, and it comes out like the children we were. I shall continue, I think, as if to a stranger. I feel a great need, after all this time, to make it separate from me. To say, "Yes, I did do that, and that, but look: there was all this time before, all this time after. Here it is on these pieces of paper. You can pick them up, you can take them away. They are not me. I am over here; far, far away; over here."

Maybe if there'd been a trial. But there was no trial. Only silence. Everyone was advised not to mention your name to me. Not even your name.

Pamelump's dad was very rich. Almost a millionaire. When his baby got born without arms or legs, he set up a trust fund for her so she could have everything she needed, or at least everything money can buy, which is not the same thing. She got all the gadgets, the attendants, the electronics but, after a while, she started to say no, because it was against her Philosophy. Lot of people offering her the stuff didn't think no-arms-no-legs people had a right to their very own Philosophy and should be grateful for all that hardware which was going to make their pitifully amputated lives that much more bearable.

"When I say I'm Pamelump, they say that's a wicked joke, calling attention to my poor affliction, 'stead of showing what a keen mind I have. Maybe being limbless has sharpened my wits, had I thought of that? I don't see them sawing the arms off their own daughters; rather go down on their knees and thank the Lord. If they won't call me Pamelump, they only think of me as the poor afflicted."

"Wendy," Pamelump's mother began on the drive home, "do you like coming to see Pamela?"

"Yes," I said. I tried to remember not to chatter. When I chattered to my mother about Pamelump, she said it wasn't natural, and then I'd have to play more British bulldog till she got over it.

"You don't have to come. I hope your mother doesn't make you?"

"Oh no, Mrs Geldenhuys. She thinks I come a bit too often."

"And what do you think, Wendy? Sometimes when I'm writing letters I hear the two of you laughing and I think how nice that you're friends."

She didn't say: "How wonderful", as if neither of us deserved friends. And she didn't say "How nice for Pamela" as if her daughter shouldn't aim so high.

"Mrs Geldenhuys," I said, my heart beating almost in my throat, "Pamelump is my best friend. My Very Best."

The charcoal burners' smoke drifted across the road so she couldn't turn to look at me.

"I'm glad," she said. "I wondered if I ought to let her go. You know, there's a special school in Jo'burg."

"She'd miss me," I said.

"Yes," said Mrs Geldenhuys, "I think she would. We did visit the school, but I don't think she liked it."

"No," I said passionately, "Pamelump's better than them."

I didn't mean 'a better person'. When Pamelump came back, she told me she had worse handicaps, but could do more, than anyone else there. They sort of flopped and let themselves be afflicted because all the helpers thought, 'yes, that's how the afflicted should be.'

"Is 'Pamelump' a nickname you have for her?"

"Yes."

"Doesn't sound very kind."

"No."

"For a very best friend, it sounds distinctly cruel. What does Pamela say about it?"

"Why don't you ask her, Mrs Geldenhuys?"

"I'm asking you, Wendy."

"She told me to call her 'Pamelump', and if I think a lump's a bad thing, I shouldn't play with her."

Next day I went to Pamelump's straight after school. We were going swimming. I didn't tell my mum because she wouldn't think Pamelump could; and if she knew, she wouldn't think Pamelump should. Miss Mbata came with us; she stayed on the side to make sure nothing happened to Pamelump. The pool on the Geldenhuys farm is behind a mulberry grove, which means you get mulberries floating in it. It also means you're completely hidden from the house. Pamelump wears a life jacket for swimming, though she has to stay on her back. She says she just loves being out of doors with no clothes on, floating up and down the little ripples of the pool, watching the trees sway and the berries drop. She moved about quite easily; her back was very strong. She sort of rocked. I was proud of the swimming because it was my idea. I dived underneath her and she had to guess where I'd turn up; she rocked over to where she thought the next mulberry would fall and tried to catch it on her life jacket.

She let me pull her round the pool by her arm stump. When she suggested it, I felt so strange, like I wanted to cry. Or burst. She hated the other kids staring at her, always wanting to prod, feel how the skin tucked in; and now here she was, asking me. I knew it was just a game in a swimming pool, but I felt like doing ten somersaults.

"What you looking at?" she asked.

"You," I said, "your mouth's all red with berries, like kissing."

She turned sideways on the life jacket, picked up a berry and blew it at me. It got me on the cheek and splattered. We laughed and I took hold of her stump and we started to whirl off across the pool, making the water rush up over the edge. We charged round and round till we were taking the water with us and it made a tide that carried us on even after I'd stopped running. I looked down at Pamelump to see if she was still laughing. She looked adorable with the mulberry stain and I bent down towards her, not knowing yet what I was going to do. I still held her stump in my hand, and she seemed so trusting and happy that I kissed her, right there where her arm ended.

I felt all her muscles go hard. What a terrible liberty. She hated being mauled or slobbered over. She'd think it was pity and never let me near her again.

"You kissed me," she said.

"Yes," I said.

"Why?"

"I wanted to," I said, "I just wanted to."

Pamelump was quiet, weighing things up. She had to plan more than me. I waited. Then I looked round to Miss Mbata, but she waved so I don't think she'd seen.

"I'm glad," said Pamelump finally.

I beamed. I hadn't expected as much as that.

The water was still moving lazily along in the swirl I'd made. We let it float us around, both on our backs, hand to stump.

"Wendy! Pamela!" It was Mrs Geldenhuys. Pamelump looked furious when her own name was called second.

"What are you two doing? Wendy, I expect this was your idea."

"No," said Pamelump, "I suggested it this time. We asked Miss Mbata to watch us and . . ."

"I'm appalled," said Mrs Geldenhuys, "absolutely appalled. Don't you know how dangerous it is? What if Pam fell onto her face before Miss Mbata could reach her? What would you do, Wendy? Would you know what to do?"

"What makes you think I'm crazy as well as a cripple?" Pamelump screamed, "I can swim, you know, just because you don't let me . . ."

By now Miss Mbata had come round our side of the pool.

"I'm very sorry, Mrs Geldenhuys," she said. "It'll never happen again. It was such a hot day and I thought there'd be no harm if she wore the life jacket and I was watching."

"You should have asked, Miss Mbata. I do not pay my servants to decide my daughter's welfare behind my back. We will speak of this later."

"She didn't decide," Pamelump spluttered, "why won't you listen? I begged her."

Mrs Geldenhuys looked half terrified, half proud. She wheeled her daughter back into the house. "Now listen, you two: that was a dangerous, stupid trick to play. It might be safe enough for you, Wendy, but Pamela has to take more precautions. In future, if you want to go in the pool, Miss Mbata will go in the water with you, and you'll ask Benjamin to watch from the side. Have you got that?"

We nodded.

"And Pamelump, I don't want to see you taking advantage of the goodwill of the servants."

When Mrs Geldenhuys had gone, I turned to Pamelump. "She's going to let us swim."

"And she called me 'Pamelump'!"

Next time I went to Pamelump's, she told me we weren't going to play anything. She had to talk to me. I settled down on the front stoep, next to her chair. She liked sitting there on her own, watching the bougainvillea.

"I want to die," she said.

"Why?"

"Because I'm getting older."

"That's no reason."

"People like me don't live past puberty."

"Then why do it yourself? Anyway you might . . ."

"I don't want to be an exception. It's only going to get worse. I'll have to hire nurses to do everything for me when I'm grown up."

"I like doing things with you."

"But you'll get tired, Wendy. You can't hang around me the rest of your life. Lifting me in and out of swimming pools, feeding me, washing me."

"If you were someone else, you wouldn't think like you do. Anyone can dive and play British bulldog."

"Except me."

"It's nothing special."

"Unless you can't do it."

She paused.

"Do you only like me cos I can't move?"

"I like you because I have more fun with you than with anyone else."

"Well it's not enough. For me, it's not enough. You the only friend I have, Wendy. I'm surprised I wasn't smothered at birth."

"Don't be silly."

"It's not silly. I have nothing to live for."

"Mulberry trees," I said, "and bougainvillea and the water lapping under you."

"I can't get to them."

"And me, Pamelump, you like me."

Pamelump was so quiet she scared me.

"It's not enough."

"I'm not enough?"

"No."

Another silence.

"You'll leave me, Wendy."

"No, never . . ."

"Already."

"What do you mean?"

"My mother called you first. You the normal one, so it must be your idea."

"But that time it was."

"You said 'let's go swimming', as if it was that simple for me. I had to do the planning."

"You always do the planning."

"So it doesn't count."

"Pamelump, I have arms so, when I'm with you, I do the things you can't. I don't know what it's like not to have arms; you have to plan it."

"Well I can't die unless you help me. Will you help?"

"That's a terrible thing to ask."

"Probably. But will you help me?"

"No."

"Wendy, every other human thing makes one choice. Whether to go on living. I can't choose, because I can't kill myself."

"How would you do it?"

"Sleepers. You must give me some of my mother's sleeping pills while no one is with us."

"What about the servants? And Miss Mbata?"

"Afternoon off Wednesday."

"Your nurse?"

"For christ's sake, can't I even die without worrying what everyone will feel about my poor, afflicted body?"

I didn't believe her. I didn't want her to die because then I ought to die too, and I wasn't finished living yet. The sun on my back and ripe mangoes in the grass, it was enough. Why wasn't it enough for her? Because we were different. Because she could not ignore her mother's orders and sneak off to the pool by herself. Whatever we did, I had two arms and two legs and she had none. But when I kissed her, I thought it might be alright. That she might let me do things for her, agree to go on living. It wasn't such a bad world. I was furious. What made her think she could go off and leave me? Why wasn't I enough?

"Will you help me?" she asked again.

I nodded. "I'll get the pills, but I'm not feeding you. It's murder."

I was eleven years old and I was very clear about murder. But that wasn't the reason. I didn't want her to die, why the hell should I have wanted to kill her?

— Pamelump, are you listening?

"I can't feed myself," she said crossly, "you know that."

"I'll put them where you can reach. If you really want to do it, you'll find some way."

"Prove myself?" she said.

She might only be playing right now, but if she got depressed again, she might do it in a fury without really meaning to. I went to her mother's room and took pills from different bottles so it wouldn't notice.

"If you take too many, it doesn't work," she said, "there was a man in the papers."

We tried to work it out, but we didn't really have a clue. I left the pills on her reading lectern.

Next day Mrs Geldenhuys rang my mother's work.

"Wendy darling, Pamela's had an accident. Smashed up her poor face. Mrs Geldenhuys says she'd love to see you."

Pamelump was all puffy with bruises and cuts. She had a black eye, but, much worse, she had knocked out two front teeth and split her tongue open. That was drastic. She needed her teeth for so many things and false ones would just fall out if she tried to pull a string with them. Her tongue was too sore to press buttons, though it would've healed in time. Her hair hung over her eyes, a bad sign. She was always arguing with her mum to cut it. It was thick and long, gave visitors something nice to exclaim over. 'What lovely hair.' Don't notice the slab in the bed. Pamelump complained that, as she couldn't push it away behind her ears, she'd rather it wasn't there to torment her. They compromised and she always had it in a plait. Now it just flopped.

I was shocked. She looked beaten, just lying back on her cushions crying.

"I'm sorry, Pamelump, I'm so sorry."

"Now do you see?" Her voice was thick. "I can't do anything. I've smashed two teeth and I can hardly talk."

She looked at me, one eye half-closed, one piercing.

"Wendy, I'm begging you. You kissed me because you love me."

I nodded.

"Please give me those pills. I fell out of my chair trying to get them."

I was angry and deserted and hurt, but I still did not want to die. Most of the pills spilled into a video case when the chair tipped; in the fear for Pamelump no one had noticed. I picked them out and held them in the palm of my hand. I would give them, one by one, to Pamelump whose mouth hurt so much she could hardly swallow. Twenty of them. I must dip my fingers into my cupped hand twenty times and feed her as I'd fed her hundreds of times before. If she wanted to change her mind, she could stop before any one of the pills.

"For pity's sake, Wendy," she said, after the third mouthful, "its not a game."

So I gave her the rest four at a time to make it quicker.

"Wait with me," she said.

I stroked her hair and kissed her. I was eleven years old, nearly twelve. I knew that she would die and that I had killed her. That no one would ever understand. Anything. Why I loved her. Especially not that. I would never see her again. Never talk to her again. Never play another moving game or swim in the pool. And I would never be able to speak to anyone else about her. They would talk of murder and affliction and what is now called euthanasia; they would not talk about the terrible loneliness, about my lack of power: I could not, for all my efforts, make a world she wanted to live in. She would see the bougainvillea waving on the stoep; she could not touch it.

I have written this just as I remember. When Pamelump closed her eyes, I waited a long time. Then I went out onto the stoep and began to pick bougainvillea. I left them on Pamelump's window sill.

5½ CHARLOTTE MEWS

"Base to Lizzy. Base to Lizzy. Over."

Middle of New Oxford Street. Damn the bloody radio. Impossible to stop now. Have to edge into the kerb, just when she'd achieved the right-hand lane.

"Base to Lizzy. Base to Lizzy. Crackle. Lizzy, Lizzy, Lizzy. If you hear me, love, give us a couple of rogers. Over."

Left foot on pavement. Right arm round parcel.

"Lizzy to Base. Lizzy to Base. Over."

"Lizzy did you pick up at Tiger?"

"Roger. Parcel On Board. Over."

"POB? Ace. Pick up: Terracotta; Drop: Charlotte Mews."

"Pick up: Roger. Crackle, crackle Mews?"

"Proceed to pick up, then RTB. Over."

"Roger rog. Over and out."

Damn and blast. Lizzy did not want to RTB. Not yet. Must be more traffic somewhere. Her daysheet counted 13 drops total. You needed at least 15 for breakeven. Kit, the controller, was paying her back. Lizzy was sure of it. Yesterday Lizzy'd totalled 26 drops, no cancellations, no returns, no waiting. 20 was average for the men, though the longterms expected 30. That's how Fast Buck made money. Kept the multidrops for the longterms, metered the rest out to the bleeps: rarely more than 15 a day. Breakeven. The odd lucky streak thrown in to make you go on playing. Keep your body out of the doorways. Just another way of using it, really. Course you weren't meant to know you were being metered. Meant to accept you weren't fast enough, unfamiliar with the streets. Then there was the bleep problem. All you knew was that somebody, somewhere wanted a drop. But to find the pick up you had to dismount, locate a functional phone box, wait your turn in the consequent

95

queue, and ring base. The radios just coasted to the kerb and called in. But a complete set cost £200 so was only allocated to the over 20s. Neat.

Yesterday Lizzy had raced wildly for 10 hours in the oozing rain. When you stay wet long enough your rubbers mush, your fingers are anyway too cold to pull the levers and your toes cramp permanently in their clips. Water no longer falls from the sky, but seeps up out of the treacherous earth. Lizzy had crashed reds, let alone ambers; shortcut pavements; been smacked in the mug by a taxi-driver for burning the Wardour one-way. She had literally not stopped all day. Ate a Mars bar at Paddington Red Star, but that's all there'd been time for. She wanted to break the 20 a day barrier and achieve a radio. Get up to 30 like the longtermers. Prove she could do it.

Most of the bleeps were women. Fast Buck was an Equal Opportunity Employer. Besides, some firms preferred a pretty packet. Handed you three skimpy slide boxes and asked sweetly, "Can you manage? We were expecting . . . someone bigger." Loaded you down with so many videos you thought the Times bag would split, then shoved their latest catalogue at you. "Might as well take this while you're at it. Saves paying twice." They liked to think of you weighted down by video nasties, labouring up narrow flights, dropping to their client, a sweating, panting face sandwiched between *Lesbian Lusts* and *Meat Cleaver Fever*. Cinema drops were the worst. As you chained up you saw the women in hot pants and goose pimples, dancing in doorways as if they'd just been walking past, heard the music and were bopping along. While you waited on the buzzer, you could hear them talking to men.

"How bout some fun, honey? Want a good time? What do you like? Black, huh, you like black? We got black, we got white, got allsorts. Got anything you want."

The bleeps rarely mentioned it to each other, but it must happen to all of them. They all had to drop to Soho. Lizzy smiled at the woman dancing. A ghastly smile, knowing that's where she'd end up if she failed at the 15 a day; that's where many of the bleeps came from. Jiggling in a doorway. Though the greenfield drops lent you the ambiguous respectability of the suburbs, when you dragged yourself panting up the steep stairs of Windmill Street, you got to be part of it anyway. That kind of place.

And it slowed you down. "Lucky little saddle." "Try this for thighs." "You do go all the way?" "Nice firm crossbar there between your legs." Lizzy ignored it, but it slowed you down. Couldn't do a racing start with the men jeering about throwing a leg over. She was fast though. When Kit turned excitedly from the phones and announced, "Okay, everybody. 7 minute drop. BJ, you on?" Lizzy was sure she could have done it. Beat a lot of the men anyway on the flat, plus she was a Londoner and hers was a racer. Even the quickest amongst them took ten minutes on a puncture. Lizzy had replaced her wheels with sprints so when she got a flat she just ripped off the old tube and stretched on a new. 2 mins max. Spent the evenings sewing up tyres, but it made the job more lucrative.

The other bleeps were more ladylike than Lizzy. Weren't going to push themselves. Smiled when the longterms asked, "How many today? Reached double figures?" You got an extra quid waiting time over 10 mins. The joke went that bleep wages were made up entirely of waiting time. So it was a point of honour not to charge it. Lizzy had sat for over half an hour in an enormous brown leather, open fire office off Saint Jameses for a bloke to sign his own cheque. Lost two drops just sitting there. "Mark it down, mark it down," the secretary hissed as Lizzy scowled. "Your young men add on at least a quid for every delivery they make." Lizzy told the other bleeps of her discovery, but they were loth to lose face. The women in Soho still danced in the doorways. Lizzy couldn't see any face to lose. It was a point of honour, also, to earn as much money as possible. Ever since, Lizzy systematically added a quid per drop.

And now she'd earned a radio. Though there were still problems. The men cut in and ripped off each other's jobs, pretending they'd heard their own name called. More serious, unless she dropped at least 20 today, Lizzy might forfeit the radio. 13 down. Another 7 to go.

She shot into Percy, dropped the Tiger, leaving her wheels unchained. Should lock up, but no time. Rain'd most probly put them off. Damp saddle. Wet bottom. On to the Terracotta pick up and . . . where was the drop? She could

97

not remember. Mind blank. Panic. Have to radio Base. They'd all hear and Kit would laugh, "Der, where I am going please, Miss?" in her hoarse whiskey voice.

When Lizzy first rang for a job, she was convinced Kit was a man. Then that she was a dyke. Such a deep voice. She must mean to have such a voice.

"So you wanna work for Fast Buck?" Kit had asked, "How long you been riding?"

"Since I was 4."

"Long time. How well dyou know London? The Soho parallelogram?"

"Enough to know it's not one."

"Unparalleled, huh? Name?"

"Anne Smith."

"Got one of those already. You'll need a name for the radio."

Not that Kit planned to give her a radio. Just a new name. It was her thought up 'Lizzy', 'Lizzy Longacre'. Which, for a 10 hour a day rider, has its little sarcasm.

Kit was a bloody good controller. 6 phones at once, 20 riders and never fucked up.

"And if I do, I admit it. That's the first thing. Send the next rider out with a big bottle of whiskey and apologise abjectly. Like this is absolutely unprecedented in the annals of the firm."

Lizzy wondered why Kit offered her these tips. She was sure as hell never going to work up to controller. Not unless she married, position of trust like that. But at first Kit clearly singled Lizzy out to talk to. Smoothed Lizzy's short, spikey hair so the bristles rubbed her palms silkily; called her hedgehog; told her she was hyper and that was a good thing.

"They say I'm hyper. Only way to be if you got a job to do, and I got 6."

Lizzy liked Kit. If she worked 10 hours, Kit worked 14. She was there doing the accounts, billing clients, working out daysheets, long after the riders had left. She personally checked the radios, re-charged batteries, replaced faulty sets. And she knew the London one-ways like the veins in her wrist. "Down Dean, up Wardour," she would remind Lizzy, when Lizzy was offering to burn them, "aint you got no pride?" She never told you wrong addresses, and she always knew what floor. If she and Lizzy had fallen out, it was not because Kit metered jobs.

Kit used to help Lizzy. Gave her returns, which doubled your takings if not your prestige. Got her doing paperwork in the slack to round up the pounds. Told her about the old country where it was hot and light. Slowly Lizzy's totals had crept up. 13, 15, 19. So, unlike many bleeps, she didn't pack up the first month in despair.

Then came That Friday. Friday was always worst, because of the weekend looming. Rushes to take to labs, bank drafts to deliver, even contracts to get signed. The funny drops: a piece of liver for the ICA, green test tubes for Regent's Park zoo, always seemed to come on a Wednesday, but Friday was one endless scurry. No one took Friday off, not even the newest, most despairing bleep. That Friday was full of panicking bosses sending manic memos to Ms Smith across town, pick ups from one firm only two floors above the drop, but none of their staff could be spared the lift time. Multidrops of urgent minutes going out to 60 Members of the Board. The later it got, the angrier and more abusive were the clients. Lizzy delivered a manilla envelope to an editing firm only to have it ripped up in front of her.

"Tell him it can't be done. It's not reasonable. He simply can't use me like this. Offer a 7 day service, they want it tomorrow. Offer 24 hours, they want it yesterday."

"Oh they all want it yesterday," agreed Lizzy philosophically, sensing a return and even a wait, during which she could eat her cheese roll.

"Well it's not possible!" shrieked the client in a rage, stamping his foot on the shredded envelope. A comic figure, a clown to amuse other clients with, but Lizzy knew a moment of terrible fear as she glanced at the intercom, checking she knew how to let herself out, away from the crazy.

"Will that be all?" she asked politely, edging for the door. But the man had calmed down, rang whoever and arranged to do the job if Lizzy would wait. Lizzy had now no desire to wait whatsoever, but it looked like the only chance she'd have to sit down all day. To refuse a drop was tantamount to resignation, and the more tired you were, the less likely to look out for side streets, homocidal maniacs, motorbikes cutting you up, the more likely to kiss a juggernaut. The man went off to deal with the editing and Lizzy sank into a deep green sofa, soft enough to cajole the most important deal; helped herself to filter coffee and read advertising awards. She gained an hour and a half, only rider to get any break at all, consequently the only one with any speed left in her. Kit's voice on the phone was hoarser and deeper than ever.

About 7 pm it began to calm down. Kit sent a couple of longterms out to get crates of beer for the riders. "Thank you everyone," she said warmly, "we've all had one helluva day and I think we've deserved these." The men knocked back the beer in approval, fizzed it up and frothed it out in a merry shower. Neither Kit nor Lizzy touched the stuff. Kit looked exhausted. On the phone for 15 hours non-stop. Responsible for 20 riders. Hundreds of drops.

"You look dead beat," said Lizzy, looking at her.

"I am, love, I am," said Kit, looking back.

"Tough job."

"Tough cookie!" Kit laughed. "Could do with a rest yourself."

"I know," said Lizzy, "I'm going greenfields with my girlfriend this weekend."

And that's when it changed. Kit with the husky voice, would flirt with Lizzy, of the bristly hair, but if Lizzy was a real dyke Kit didn't wanna know. Or maybe Kit wanted to be butch and Lizzy's sympathy galled. Was it butch to ride flat out and flex your thighs; femme to control the riders, send out for beer for the lads? Sounded right. Only Kit was tall, strong, loud-mouthed and unemotional. Lizzy was little, lithe, nervy and squeaky-voiced. Well, maybe Kit was pissed off Lizzy already had a lover. Not that that should have worried her. They hadn't lasted the weekend. But Kit never said. Just stopped giving Lizzy any but the longest drops, at the end of an underpass with a shortcut via the motorway.

On her first day with a radio, Lizzy did not want to call base for a repeat transmission. She'd done the Tiger, picked up from Terracotta and now where? Oh shit. Return to Base. No chance of another job for half an hour. Put her out of the running. But surely there'd been an address given out before the crackles. Had one of the men cut in on her? Useless, as she was POB and they weren't. Lizzy hated to think Kit liked the slimey creatures; called them 'Yes, my sweet,' and 'Yes, my love.' Aberrant: that big, husky woman with the cheekbones and the jaw chatting up men, of all people. The motor bikes in the leather and zips were femme; the pedals, with black tights and condor vests were clearly butch. They were the ones with muscles and a penchant for raw steak. Or perhaps Lizzy'd got it wrong again. Couldn't work out butch and femme for women, let alone them.

It was no good. Charlotte Street already and she could not remember the drop.

"Lizzy to Base. Lizzy to Base. Come in Base. Over."

"Crackle. Crackle. Nyarrzzemd."

"Lizzy POB in Charlotte Street. Lizzy, Charlotte Street, Parcel on Board."

"Nyarzz. Static. Splutter."

"Lizzy? Base here. $5\frac{1}{2}$ Charlotte Mews."

"Repeat. Repeat drop. Sounded like Charlotte Mews? Over."

But the radio was dying, if not dead. Trust Kit to give her flat batteries. And she had trusted Kit. Pathetic. But taking directions from Kit used to be pure joy. So beautifully accurate, lyrical almost. "South along Berwick. West Noel. South Poland. East Darblay. Right at Portland Mews. Yellow doorway, left arch, top buzzer. And return via Hyde. It's hot and you'll like the water fountain."

Lizzy twiddled the buttons. White noise, more static, then:

"Okay everybody. Well I'm very pleased to introduce myself: I'm Nyarrzzemd and I shall be one of your 4 encouragers during your time at Charlotte Mews. This is what you might call an 'orientation speech', in which I shall introduce a few basic concepts, which may be of use to you in your journey. If you do not feel you can use any encouragement at the present moment, please do not hesitate to turn off. Invert journeyings can be as productive as out and outs."

Lizzy reckoned she could do with some encouragement. She stayed tuned.

"As you already know, and as we must repeat, our knowledge of your journey is sketchy in the extreme. We cannot advise you concretely, except in terms of how best to pit yourselves against adversity. We do not know, however, what constitutes adversity for you. We will ask you to push your muscles to, through, and past breaking point and not break, so that at every moment you are both acheing and sinking into pain, transcending pain. You will run till your lungs can no longer gasp, your legs no longer pound nor your feet feel the ground under you. You will swim till your back longs to become a dolphin, or at least a hinge, till the battle to breast the water is almost lost. You will ride till your hands shake and your fingers twitch from clutching, till the ball muscles in your calves harden into marble and your thighs are long, lean tendons of pushing. Only you will know whether you can go on or not, because, when you go forth, only you will be able to secure yourselves from danger. We will urge you to continue. You must be strong enough to tell us to stop.

"You must prepare yourselves for tremendous depression, also, lethargy, fear, misery, confusion and here we can offer you only exercises in extreme sensory deprivation of a kind you have hitherto not imagined. From what little we know of the journey you are about to undertake, from those few survivors willing to testify, the place to which you are going seems almost to emanate anguish from its roots. These emanations are, of course, traceable to concrete causes by one qualified to judge. You will not be so qualified.

I hope the following illustrations will give you some idea what to expect of the exercise at least, if not the reality beyond. You are lying in bright sunlight beneath a cloudless sky, the flowers around you the usual mix of azalea translucent and lush tropical. You are thirsty and stand up in search of a glass of water. You go into the house and it's so dark in there, after the light outside, that you are blinded by the gloom. You can see nothing, but walk through the room with your fingertips. Slowly your eyes become used to the dimness and pick out the shadowy outline of familiar objects, begin almost to see a certain beauty in a comparison of greys. Now, hold still at that point. Your eyes, used to the dark, will lose their capacity to appreciate bright colours, will think them gaudy and shy away. Will no longer distinguish between the fresh lime, the deep viridian and the flashing emerald of our native hills. Will call them simply green, tolerate them at dusk only.

Again, you are lying in bright sunlight beneath a cloudless

sky, the sun swarms over your naked body suffusing it with warmth. You feel a slight tightening in your cunt from the simple caress of the sun's rays lazily playing upon it. You do not wish to burn, so reach out for some light garment beside you. Slowly, you dress. And with each article of clothing you feel colder and colder and pile on more clothes in search of warmth till, finally, you are muffled under thick sweaters and woollen vests, enormous overcoats and fur-lined gloves, boots on your feet making your steps heavy and awkward, your ears covered in a long knitted scarf so you can scarcely hear. Gone are the bare toes skipping lightly on sand, running luxurious in velvet grass. Now you walk sombrely, and others like you, bumping against each other, hardly hearing, and with no idea even of the shape of your own bodies.

Once more you are lying in bright sunlight beneath a cloudless sky, you are eating peaches. Peaches and cherries, nectarines, plums, tangerines and grapes. They are firm, sweet, soft, juicy, wet. You spit out pips with strong teeth and much laughter. You reach for another. There are none left. There is only custard. Cold custard. Cold, long-congealed and slightly burnt, slightly powdery, as though with lumps of mixture not smoothed in. You say you don't like custard. Then there is tinned tomatoes, raw chick peas. You stand up to dance at least, if you cannot eat. The band plays a waltz, sweet, old-fashioned. You like to waltz, but your partner does not keep time and will not touch you, will only jerk spasmodically with grim heroism, hands in pockets. Frantically you look at the pictures on the walls for some soothing symmetry, a flash of energy, a hint of purpose. They are hung slightly crooked. For no reason. It would have been as easy to hang them straight. But they are not. The colours do not clash, they edge uneasily away from one another. There is no vigour in the brush strokes but an apologetic, helpless dash from place to place which peters out ineffectually.

Finally, across the room you glimpse an old friend, a close friend with whom you have spent long, intense hours talking, persuading, earnestly, happily. You make your way towards her through the heavy, muffled figures in the gloom. You will tell her how it is always cold here, how, when the sun shines, it is brief and watery, the colours muted and everything tastes of cold, wet custard, slightly sweet. How women dance out of time, the graphics slope off-centre and even the purples and oranges do not clash but sidle. Everything will be bearable if only you two can agree on the clammy, spongelike awfulness. She tells you to cheer up and make the best of it, the cold is not so much harsh as bracing. You'll get used to it, you may even go swimming, give your body to the waves. She giggles. She never used to giggle. She says she likes cold custard, that grey's a very subtle taste, co-ordinates so well with pink. You look out bleakly at the oily sea. She puts a sympathetic hand on your shoulder and tells you, you must try to enjoy it a little. You must not feel so passionately, this is a world of men, a world where women care for men, and for men it is neither possible, nor advisable, to feel passion.

Well, this has just been an introductory presentation and I feel it is only fair to ask you all, if only for formality's sake, whether any of you are the least put off by what you have heard. Do please speak now, your niggling doubts, your slightest uncertainties. No one is obliged to go on the journey. So, are you all still committed?"

Crackle. Splutter. Criik. Whoosh. Sh, sh.

Then another voice began to speak, and another, till there came the sound of many voices speaking together.

"No. No. We're not. Sounds terrible. Perfectly dreadful. Who in her right mind would want to go to a place like that? No wonder they go crazy."

Then the first voice came back.

"I fully accept your reasoning. Your sentiments are mine exactly. But every generation we have to put the question, in case anyone tunes in and feels something is being kept from her."

Crackle. Crackle. Static interference. And Lizzy's radio fell silent.

"Base to Lizzy. Base to Lizzy. Come in please. Over."

"Lizzy here. Over," called Lizzy, dazed at the sound of Kit's voice.

"Current location? You were told to RTB. Over."

"Sorry, I . . . I . . Kit, didn't you hear that broadcast?"

"What broadcast? Specify. Over."

"From Charlotte Mews."

"Repeat transmission station. Over."

"$5\frac{1}{2}$ Charlotte Mews. It was . . ."

"I know what it was! Message received and understood. So they're back on air. Has it been that long? There was just a chance with you, but you seemed more concerned with drops, I wasn't sure."

"Unsure of what? Specify uncertainty. Over."

"That they'd get through to you."

"To me? They were transmitting to each other. Whole different system. Over."

"You got tuned, believe me."

"How do you know? Specify certainty. Over."

"This journey they were talking about. That's here. I took it."

"You mean it's not like this there? Weather conditions hot, light, sunny, permanent fixture? Over."

"Affirmative."

"So why the hell did you leave, Kit? Weren't taken in by that transcending pain shit?"

"Negative. Kept receiving Outside Broadcasts. Sounded like a lot of power men had. Deciding, striding, conquering. Hot stuff. Never occurred to me I'd have to be a woman. Over."

"Women in the Mews don't have power? Over."

"Affirmative power. Negative work ethic. Over."

"Negative work ethic? They got no traffic? Over."

"Double affirmative. Traffic but no deadlines. Love affairs instead. Over."

"Could speed em up. Good love affair."

"Possibility."

"Want to try it?"

"Meet you down there, darling."

"Message received and understood. Proceeding Charlotte Mews. Estimated arrival time $2\frac{1}{2}$ mins. Weather conditions fair to exuberant. Over and Out."

EATING PEOPLE IS WRONG

Averil's bedroom was thirteen feet long and ten feet wide.
She lived alone. On the left they played non-stop reggae,
very loud. On the right they played smooch, low but
insistent. Her office was roughly the same dimensions as her
room. She shared it with a colleague. The office on the left
played non-stop sixties, forty-eight by forty-eight. The office
on the right played radio one, to an endless supply of nearly
flat batteries. The walls were breeze block. Averil bought
herself a walkbod and a blank cassette.

She had been hired for her ability to type the same letter
fifteen types in minor variations and without complaining. If
her boss wrote "and so we see that people who take time off
to have babies . . .", Averil refrained from correcting 'people'
to 'women' as so many secretaries would have done. She was
paid not to think. She was certainly not paid to think. Not
on University time.

Once Zoe pinned a memo to a pile of term papers.

"What do you think about Women's Studies, Averil?"

Averil typed back, neatly,

"Women's Studies make me feel like I'm being eaten."

Zoe stormed into the office, eyes sparkling with enthusiasm, and insisted,

"But what do you **think**, Averil?"

"Uses up a lot more tissues than Geology."

"Are women so fragile?"

"With the geology men, I made sure to buy rainbow pastel
Kleenex so they'd only bother me if they were really
dripping. Your women take anything going."

Averil had applied for the job because, unlike Geology,
Women's Studies was right on the edge of campus. Zoe had
complained at the interview that they were too far from the

postroom to use the university franking machine and Averil would have to buy in stamps. Real ones with sticky backs. Averil's great joy was her stamp arranging. She was the only woman in living memory who had managed to persuade the British Post Office to send her each new compendium a month in advance of a price rise. A widely advertised service, nearly impossible to tap. Averil would pore over the list of new denominations. Then she would collect stamp rinds, those thin white frames round each sheet with a neat block of colour along the right hand edge, exactly matching the stamps it has framed. One rind for each denomination. When she came to send out letters, she typed fast and mindless, plotting the while what colour combination she would try on the envelope. Her preference was for foreign destinations. The higher the price, the more possibilities. Parcels were a great plus, the big pound stamps adding size as a consideration. She wondered sometimes, when she had completed a particularly subtle toning of greens into blues across the top of a jade laid to the States, (the airmail sticker gracefully accentuating the lightness of the tones) whether anyone noticed and even enjoyed her designs. The ephemeral nature of envelope art lent it the status of a gratuitous act, if you discount personal satisfaction, which she rather thought she did.

"Ms V. Chowdry," she murmured to herself, crossing the name off the list of new students, "Wonder what the V. stands for."

"Oh!" Veera exclaimed, picking a slim ivory envelope up off the mat, decorated with a single pale green stamp and two, dove grey '5 pence to pay' stickers, "Such elegance to come through my mail box. Fortuitous beauty, like stray sunlight on wet mud."

V. stood for Veera, though Veera was not her name. At her English boarding school, in the first class, on the first day, upon polite enquiry, she had announced that she was called Verity, Amrit, Jyoti, Nan Chowdry, her mother being eclectic in tendency. The polite English teacher had begged her to speak more slowly, she was not used to Indian names. Veera had repeated it, and the English teacher spelled everything correctly, save Verity, which, she claimed, she could not pronounce. Veera told her it was an English name. The teacher assured her it was not, offering 'Vera' as a compromise, with an extra 'e', to remind herself it was Indian.

The women in Veera's village always gave their children two names. One for the world, and the English and school; one for the family. As soon as they were old enough, the children picked a name for themselves, which they told no one. It was their very special magic name. A bond stronger than blood or sex or hatred to offer someone your name in exchange for theirs. In India Veera's family were above such simple superstition; here in complacent England, it had its uses.

Averil released the second letter from the machine. It was one of those new, rather disconcerting typewriters which refuses to allow you any hand in the matter. It swallowed the paper up, positioned it for you and beeped angrily if you overshot your margins. In the cavity under the cover, where it ought to have concealed its innards, was nothing but a small green box. Averil was able to store her walkbod in the resultant void.

"Janet Kay Morris," read the second envelope, (blue and purple on vellum).

"Here, Kay, you've got one too," shouted Veera.

Each woman had planned special kindness to the other, to make up for being accepted where her lover was not. Now both had made the course. Anti-climax. No furious, soothing, "They simply don't appreciate you! I don't understand how they can take me and refuse you. There's no justice." The first stirrings of contempt for a university so easy to get into.

On the way up, Veera rushed through the last text on the reading list, a thing about welfare and the family. She would not waste educational time catching up on background. Kay alternately gazed at the waterlogged fields and dipped affectionately into the latest Molly Keane.

The man opposite pulled in his enormous legs, stopped drumming on his thigh, and stood up to reach his coat. Chelmsford. As the train pulled away again and charged off towards Colchester, Veera began to feel funny. She swallowed, pressed her lips together and said,

"Colchester, next stop."

"Mmm," said Kay from rural Ireland.

"We'll have to get out of the train and walk along the street."

"Take the bus," muttered Kay.

"Which bus?"

"Whichever bus goes to the University."

"You don't know, do you?"

"We can ask."

Veera stared out the window. In it were reflected a family with two daughters. The younger was cuddled up against her mother.

"Soon be there," said mother, stroking darling's hair.

"I'm dying to stretch my legs."

How easy.

"Come on!" said Kay, "The big adventure."

Veera stared resolutely out the window till her eyes were dry again, gulped, shoved her books in her case and gathered up the handles. They followed the other passengers along the platform, handed in their tickets and were out of the station before Veera had had time to prepare. There it was in front of her: buildings, streets, shops, traffic, with no clue to its meaning, collected only under the bland umbrella: Colchester.

"It's getting on," remarked Kay, "time we find which bus, we'll be late. Let's take a taxi."

Already, and without effort, Kay had tamed it. Was even now asserting her presence in this strange place. Tossing out 'bus' and 'taxi' with complete familiarity. But it wasn't that easy. What do taxis look like in Colchester? The word was, possibly, international, but by the time it was near enough to read, the cab would have swept past. And how to hail it, once recognised? A wave? A whistle? Only at certain well-marked points, clearly labelled for local inhabitants, perfectly inscrutable to Kay and Veera? It came fuzzily into Veera's mind that perhaps the cab would be yellow; that was the colour they were in Indonesia. Or was it New York? She struggled to concentrate. What colour were cabs in New York? Madison Avenue, her father stepping off the kerb, leaving a huddle of daughters and suitcases on the pavement. The abrasive term 'jaywalking' flashed before her. She was now so far from Colchester, so confused between a welter of place names, that the nausea, which had been building up since the train, began to constrict her stomach. She must get there as quickly as possible; sick panic would only make matters worse and frighten Kay, but the street was closing in on her, levelling out into a long thin tunnel. What she knew to be grass, and therefore green, was grey. As she tried to look beyond the tunnel, she saw that everything was black and white.

"What is it?" Kay cried in consternation, holding Veera's wrists, "for Godsake tell me what's the matter."

Veera was standing on a grass strip, tears streaming down her face, eyes squeezed shut in terror. The wrists which Kay held were shaking.

It was dangerous to stand up. Veera wanted to fall against the ground.

"Tell me what you want," cried Kay, "I want to help you."

"We have to get there. We just have to get there."

"Don't!" Kay snapped sharply, "tell me what you want."

"I'm telling you. Listen to me. We have to get there."

Kay took Veera's free arm and guided her through the streets. Veera was in Karachi, London, Bombay; with her father, Kay, her sisters, but it seemed to be alright. Wherever it was, it seemed to have a useable transport system. Possible to ask and to be understood; to move and to arrive.

They landed slap bang in the middle of the student cafeteria, where the young: handsome, greasy or earnest, sprawl and raise their little voices at each other whilst silent, bowed women collect cold, half-finished cups of coffee. A scene recognisable the world over, so that wherever in the world it was, this must be its student cafeteria. Veera and Kay sat down. Half an hour too early for wine and cheese. Veera gathered up the nausea, dizziness, lapse of colour, tunnel vision and the shakes, garlanded into symptoms, and presented them to Kay, who deserved something after her heroism with the transport network.

Yes she had had it ever since she came to England.

Yes, since she'd been a lesbian.

Yes she'd been under the doctor. Several doctors, a psychiatrist, a clinic.

Yes she sometimes lost consciousness.

Yes she could feel it coming on and yes they had suspected epilepsy. But the tests were all negative. Blood, urine, faeces, electroencephalograph; there was nothing whatever wrong with her save nausea, dizziness, lapse of colour, tunnel vision and the shakes. What a comfort.

A black woman wearing red silk and fulsome turquoise earrings
[How bright, how gaudy. Amazing what these black skins can get away with.]
meets her blonde friend with the creamy pearls,
[My Godfather adds one pearl every birthday. It's just long enough to wear round my neck now.]
for dinner in a white restaurant: bleached napery, ivory linen, silver cutlery, crystal glasses.
[No, we no longer scrub those brown babies to get the dirt off.]
The waiter takes their coats: one silver fox, one mink, and deposits them in the cloakroom. The attendant stares across at the black woman.
[These darkies. Money to burn. I ask you.]
They order in French. The waiter does not understand the black woman; the blonde friend repeats with a smile, fingering her pearls.
The black woman asks for the Ladies. Does she want to powder her nose? As she enters, two white women are touching up their lipstick. They glimpse her reflection in the mirror. One pulls her purse in nearer to her; the other puts hers away in her handbag.

Veera must learn the lie of the streets, the bus numbers, the taxi ranks; must plan her escape routes.

The therapist tried to treat the cause. The chicken tried to cross the road. The striker tried to bring down the government. Veera had to go on living.

England was a white world, but India was not, despite the Raj and a certain, fiercely denied, lingering deference to English taste. In India it was perfectly respectable to be Indian. Such shame, on Veera's family, to marry an outsider.

Across the candlelight, and over an arrangement of snowy
orchids, two women look at each other.
[Are you waiting for anyone? Ah, I see, just the two of you.]
"Excuse me, can I just squeeze. . . Thanks. Thank you."
Without looking round, the white woman shuffles her chair
forward, though this is quite unnecessary.
"Cliff, old boy! How are you? Bianca, my dear, this is Cliff.
He was with me on the Times. Well, how are you touting
your talent these days?"
"Hank! Proverbial black sheep."
The party on the left of the black woman shakes hands with
the party on her right, lightly brushing her shoulder. He has
to swing on his chair leg to do so.
The two women continue to look at each other.
"Bianca, shake hands with my old friend Cliff."
Bianca declines, an embarrassed smile to the two women.
Hank catches the smile. Gleans a message.
"What about you two ladies? On your own tonight?"

It is perfectly respectable to be a woman. It is even
possible to be two women. Naturally, however, this is a
transition state. Not a homeland.

Veera's muscles were slowly beginning to unclench but, as
she raised her cup to her lips, she saw that her hands were
still trembling. Coffee spilled onto the table, to be mopped
up later, no doubt, by one of the bowed, silent women.

"I have to go to bed, Kay. My blood's way down."

"And leave me all alone with the Marxists? Don't be so
selfish."

An old joke, that only socialists taught Women's Studies
and Kay's retort was intended lightly, but Veera wanted to
throw coffee at her. Had her hand been steady enough.

Averil smiled vacantly as Zoe provided the rest of the staff
with, if not titles, at least surnames. She was only Averil, our
secretary. Anything you need to know, just ask Averil.

Zoe beamed at the new intake, trying to fit names to them.
A mixed bag. Always a number of foreign students. Policy.

"Well, they bring in the money. With the cuts and

everything. No ceiling on foreign fees. These oil sheikhs think they're buying their daughters beauty lessons."

"You do nothing to enlighten them."

"I have to run a Women's Studies course from an underfunded Sociology department, in leaky breeze blocks, at the edge of campus. Besides. It's the women who apply; they read the prospectus. If they want to hoodwink Daddy, good luck to them."

"Discrimination."

"But this *is* England."

"What about those who can't afford it?"

"We never turn anyone away for lack of money. If they're bright and motivated, we find a way."

"Probably take one look at the fees and give up."

When Zoe tired of having this conversation with herself, she could have turned to Veera for enlightenment.

"Actually, we anglicise our names and accents so the question is not asked. Heard it before? Like not holding hands in public. Let Anglo-centrism work for us."

But Veera was in bed.

Kay was lurking nervously in a corner.

"Can I get you a glass of something?" A bouncy young woman in jeans, looked about fifteen. "I'm Sally, by the way. Were you at Sussex?"

Kay shook her head.

"It's just that everyone I've met so far was at Sussex. Cept me, of course. I was at Lancaster. Trust me to get it wrong. Silly Sally."

Kay began to feel glazed, but Sally was friendly. A boon in a roomful of strangers.

"I don't really drink," Kay said, "but if they had some orange juice."

Sally grinned, "Something to hold in your hand," fetching her a glass.

"Why did you apply here?" Kay asked.

"Oh, same as everyone. Battle weary."

At her age?

"Marching, petitioning, sitting in . . ."

They still did that, then.

Sally was looking at her. "Think that doesn't count? I've done the refuges, sleep-overs, taken the line. I'm tired.

Backlog of books to read."

Kay supposed she'd fitted in a year at Greenham too.

"How bout you?"

"I wanted a degree. This one didn't require 3 A levels."

"Aren't you a feminist, then?"

"I'm not entirely cynical."

"Living in hall?"

"No. Staying with friends."

"All year?"

"Till we buy a place. Tried house hunting from London, but it was too exhausting. You have to be on the spot."

"Gosh! Do you think that's on? Spose you must. Only a lot of people would say it was elitist. Property is theft."

"Yes. From us."

Kay was the wrong person to quarrel with about property.

When Averil put her name down for the Ethics course, Zoe was pleased but puzzled. The course had been added on after the last minute and Zoe would teach it herself, as well as a half unit on Welfare and The Family. Up till the famous last minute, an equally famous young man had been about to lecture on the social construction of sexuality. There had been ructions. First, assuming that sex was bound to be popular, Zoe had felt it safe to make the course an option. Half the students complained that their sexuality was the basis of their politics and the course must be part of the core. Second, and more raucous, what the hell was a man doing, preaching to women about sex, (again)? The famous young man had departed thankfully for his secluded niche in Sociology to issue Lacanian analyses of Foucault, Fouculdian analyses of Derrida so that, as was proper, his fame should spread and his attendance drop. He was replaced by a no-nonsense Althusserian who referred to the family as an Ideological State Apparatus (ISA) when she had to refer to it at all. ("Poor M. Althusser. Had to kill Mme Althusser. How dreadful for him.") What she liked best was to get the students talking about themselves. Participant Observation, she called it. The students liked this even less than the dear little queer. A gay man would not have had the nerve to ask what they did in bed. So Zoe, ever-sensitive, scrapped the course altogether and instituted Ethics.

And now Averil had registered. What for? Zoe wondered.

It is a little known fact about Averil, but she was not born a secretary. Her fingers are not word processors, nor her belly button a computer terminal, notwithstanding certain dazzling feats of administrative sprezzatura. (Italian for no sweat. Supergirl-the-gormless lisping prettily, "Why are you doing this?", flipping her attackers like pancakes, a hundred yards into a junk pile. An overworked secretary altering the term's timetable at the whim of her supervisor, whilst still accommodating the demands of eight other staff, thirty students and the cleaners, not once but twice, and at short notice. No sweat. You dig.) Averil is, in all respects, a perfectly normal human being. Except one. Her aversion to noise. She sees this as bad research on her part, but really, how was she to tell? In office procedure exercises they blanked out the background so you could concentrate. It seems so unlikely, doesn't it, that the Academy should need perpetual sound. Food and water, air, shelter, a place to breed, easy; but 'why do men oppress women' in every sociology course across the land? The answer to 'why' was, almost invariably, 'because he/she/they want to'. Fortunately, there is more to life than human motivation.

Averil dreamed of companionable silence which certain delicate, long-pondered words might frame, as bone china offers the fragrance of flower-scented Darjeeling.

"Why are you such a snob, Kay?" asked Sally.

"Same reason you're a slob, Sally dear," Kay replied, "trying to escape my class."

Sally felt furious. Which was a very exciting thing to feel for Kay.

Listening to the comforting silence of her walkbod, (punctuated by the little rattle swish of the wheels,) walking, maybe running, not jogging, to work (she had never mastered the Colchester bus system,) Averil decided to turn her aversion into a project:

"The Need for, and Prevalence of, Background Noise amongst Late Twentieth Century Humans with Particular Reference to Staff and Students on the Women's Study Course at Colchester University 1984-1985." Subtitled, "Towards a Feminist Anthropophagy." She would take next term's Ethics as the site of her excavations; her hypothesis would be that: rather than examine their own oppression, women's studies tutors ate their students, to a background of nonsense words, like the drums of ritual slaughter.

That settled Averil, wearying of philatelics, put her mind to philandering, most honourable of occupations, when honourably undertaken.

"Look, what about this one, Veera? 'Newly mod, two bed, large recep/diner, avocado bthrm suite wth olive splshbck. Close university and all amenities.' Only fifty thou."

"What's a splshbck?"

"Who cares? It's only the bthrm. 'Ind. gas c.h. Price to inc. carpt and crtns.' Shall we take a look?"

"We can't afford it."

"Sell the flat."

"And then where'll we live? It's only three years. Unless you've discovered reasons for staying the rest of your life?"

Kay shrugged off Veera's jealousy.

"Why don't we rent the place Averil told us about?"

"Paying rent is like buying water. If we take out a second mortgage on Dorcas Terrace, the tenants will more than cover our repayments."

"So we buy two glasses of water. Sell one to pay for the other."

"That's how it works, Veera mia, turning your nose up won't change matters."

"Oh you, always wanting someone to admire your cleverness."

Kay drove off in a fury. And what about Veera? Always found some political justificaton for what Kay knew to be pure squeamishness. Cowardice, not to put too fine a point on it. They'd made no provision for coming to Essex because Veera couldn't bear to think about it. Well, she'd made one chatty call to an old school friend, catching up on husbands, colds and children's shoe sizes, slipping in at the end that she and Kay would be students that autumn, was there anywhere. . .? So here they were in the friend's granny flat with infant prodigy, Bimsy ('not yet nine and so accomplished') demanding piano practice at eight in the morning. There was simply no room in the rest of the house so, of course, the piano was lodged in Kay and Veera's sitting room. While Veera devoted herself to her duties as student and aunty, Kay scribbled off essays, late, and scoured the papers for rooms away from the piano. Which Veera refused even to look at.

Yet it was Veera, unknowingly, who first prodded Kay into owner occupancy.

Zoe started each group with a discusson of who they were and what they hoped to get out of coming. Standard WLM practice which Zoe defended passionately to her colleagues. No one took the idea seriously enough to find anything to disagree with. It was hard, however, to avoid baiting Zoe, who saw her field as a revolutionary hotbed. Any opposition caused her to become gratifyingly emotional. It was like taking off one's clothes to exhibit real feeling in the senior commonroom.

Zoe intended her courses to be based on nothing but real feeling, equality and exchange. Like a modernday c-r group, perhaps, though she never stopped to remember that c-r groups had been neither led nor graded. She was clumsy, often, and easily shocked. When she talked about herself, the students felt embarrassed. When they talked, they felt she was using them. Intense, well-meaning and well-protected. Oh beware of those who mean you well.

"Where do you think Women's Studies fit in the Women's Liberation Movement?"

Integral as Women's Aid or Rape Crisis; more intellectual than Greenham; less dangerous than smashing porn shops. (Yes, but what about the women's liberation movement?)

"Do you want this course to change anything in your own lives?"

118

Question expecting the answer 'yes'.

(Equality, exchange: 'You want', 'your lives'. Not Zoe's.)

"I get letters after my name," said Kay, "and the estate agents have to treat me with a little more respect." She had, that morning, been left on a door step for half an hour by an agent who doubted she was worth fifty thou and had no patience with time wasters.

"Maybe I have a different attitude to learning from the rest of you," said Veera, "India has a great tradition of respect for knowledge, but it is often very hard for women to attain. Sometimes I think for an Indian woman, learning to read is liberation! I am what you call 'an ardent feminist', so I want my academic pursuits to coincide with my politics."

"Oh me too, Veera," said Sally. "When you're in the thick of it, it's like you've got no time to think anymore. I want to work out general principles, you know, discuss things in depth now . . ."

"That's ridiculous," said Veera, "like panting for a month so you can swim the Bay of Bengal underwater."

Sally smiled complicity. She liked being teased.

Veera snorted. Not only had she been misunderstood, but patronised as well.

"I want to find out about lesbians," Kay dived in gallantly after them. They were an impossible combination. Why didn't Sally simply let Veera alone; it wasn't going to work. "All the rest, the discussing and everything, I could do on my own, but I thought there might be books, I don't know, records somewhere . . ."

Zoe blushed at the word 'lesbian', but said that certainly she hoped to make resources more available to ordinary women.

Kay bridled at the word 'ordinary'. The only working class woman in the group. Well, the only one with an accent.

Sally laughed and said kindly, "That's a neat trick: discussing everything with yourself, Kay." Good old Sally.

And the conversation continued on less thorny, duller ground.

"Pregnancy Abortion Contraception stop Adoption State Provision stop Council Sales Nursery Places Single Mothers stop Working Class Aspirations Avocado Bathroom Suites Mixer Taps stop. . ."

"Kay, housing is a particular concern of yours, isn't it?"
Again! Truly, Zoe was clumsy.

"What she want? My accent and her theories? All that guff about single mothers; you'd hear it better argued in The Guardian," Kay raged at Sally as they walked by the estuary in Wivenhoe.

"Mmm," Sally groaned sympathetically, "makes you wonder who she thinks she's got in her class. I thought this was meant to be about us."

"And I thought we were meant to know more about 'us' than anyone else."

"She did ask you, though, Kay. You didn't take her up on it."

"I'm not talking about myself as if I was a social phenomenon. What I do, what happens to me, is my *life*. It hurts."

"I think she'd let you. . ."

"Try and stop her. Then she'd write it all down and tell the next group what working class women think."

"Zoe's not that bad."

"No, but I don't see her exposing herself."

"She's got more to lose."

"Perfect."

"Calm down, sweetie. It's lovely here and you're missing it."

"I'm quite calm. I'm pissed off."

"Kay, you're stomping past the darlingest little cottage; it's got windows like portholes and a grey pussycat staring out."

Kay glared round and noticed, at last, that the tide was in, there were sailing boats bobbing, and rowing boats, seagulls turning, a pink sun through the grey cold of November. They were walking a little cobbled seafront with irregular cottages, sandbags out front and slatted half-doors against the sea.

"Bijou res," laughed Sally.

"Period features and sea view. Wonder what colour the splashback is."

"The what?"

"Bath tiles. All Veera worries about."

The Prow, The Boards, Wivenhoe. What would Kay's mother say?

When she met Veera, Kay was living in a basement in Notting Hill. Her friends, whose address books she had filled, suggested she take up residence on a post office redirection form. She thought if she were dead, at least she would not have to live anywhere. The day she moved, and went to buy teas for the removal team, she passed a billboard announcing the Notting Hill rapist had struck again.

She met Veera a fortnight later at a public meeting for local women which was packed and muted. They suggested a telephone tree and a map of safe houses. Some lesbians pointed out that mixed houses were not safe. A straight woman went over the details of rapes so far: what area, which flats, what time.

"I live in North Kensington, so it won't be me, will it?"

"I live on the second floor. . ."

"I'm never on my own at night. . ."

So it won't be me. It won't be me. It can't be me. Not me. Again the lesbians pointed out that it happened all the time, no one was safe, there was no safe place. Kay agreed, but could not take her eyes off the straight woman.

"It's the communal gardens, isn't it? I've heard he hides in the communal gardens. Well I only have a window box."

For some reason, everyone laughed. Kay smiled at the straight woman, and burst into tears.

Five hundred women in an Ecumenical Hall. They divided into postcodes; exchanged addresses and phone numbers, would feel safer, in the street at least, if they knew they were passing a women's house.

"I like the rich," someone said. "Communal gardens. About as communal as their public schools."

Women looked anxious, sensing division. The straight woman sniffed and said:

"Isn't anyone else scared? I'm here because I'm terrified."

Some women smiled encouragement, others nodded tensely.

"I do get scared," someone agreed, "when I'm in the house alone. But I just do some hard thinking and get it all in perspective."

"How?" asked the straight woman.

"Oh you know. I control it."

The straight woman looked down and began to smooth the hem of her sari. Kay warmed to her. They walked home together. It was recommended.

"Thank you," said Veera, "I'm fine now. My lover's staying tonight."

Kay felt used.

"She couldn't come to the meeting," Veera explained, "had to work late."

"Oh!"

Veera looked at Kay.

"Because I wear a sari? We do it in India too, you know. All it takes is two women."

Kay smiled, ashamed. Veera stood at her gate watching Kay across the road till she disappeared into the basement.

They became friends, were in and out of each other's houses, though, curious thing, Kay began to notice Veera never used her toilet. Finally she asked why.

"It's too cold," said Veera who, mercifully, replied to questions.

Her simple statement did more than years of instability, of damp walls and crumbling plaster, leching landlords and violent neighbours: it made Kay buy her own flat.

Kay and Sally were rowing across to Fingringhoe; a boat went with The Prow, as well as the round grey pussy cat. Veera preferred to stay home. Tonight was the house-warming and she didn't want to tire herself out. Besides, what was the point of interfering? That Kay wanted Sally was what hurt. Much less painful if she merely slept with her in drunken softness. Though oh! Veera prayed she wouldn't.

Veera tried instead to think about the party: ice, spare loo paper, flashes for the camera, black olives. Kay still bought green. Veera went into the kitchen to check nothing perishable had been left on the top shelf of the fridge: it would stick to the freezer compartment and bruise. As she bent to look, knotted with misery, she heard a click at the front door. Averil.

"Okay, hold it right there. Now tell me exactly what you were thinking."

That if Kay hasn't held Sally's hand, she's wanted to; if

she hasn't pressed her lips softly to Sally's, she's wanted to; if she hasn't darted her tongue into Sally's mouth, over Sally's breasts, along Sally's clitoris, she's wanted to. All afternoon she's wanted to. If she's so much as put a fond hand to Sally's shoulder, I'll know. All through the party, the congratulations and "What a simply darling little house!", I'll know.

"About this man I met in the market."

Which was what Averil called 'perverting the course of silence'. Silence had to be wooed, prepared for, coaxed lovingly. Every time you hid from words, avoided speech when speech was necessary, you debased silence, pretended it was an easier, less precious thing. It took bitter, acheing or joyous words to reach it, a battle all the way. You could not slump and expect it to calm you; it would not, on those terms.

"I was buying fish for tonight and wondering what I would wear. Half the fun of parties used to be the dressing up. We'd all go to my elder sisters' room, decide on colours, choose saris, paint our nails and our toe nails and our faces, brush each other's hair, oil it, dress it. There's not so much to do when you're a lesbian feminist, after you've taken a bath and decided whether to wear your tie.

I was smiling at myself and gazing at a vegetable stall. I like the familiar way they write aubergines: 'obos'. There was a man standing next to me, gazing also. I caught him in the corner of my eye and turned round. He was Indian. I'm sure of it. The gestures, the way of standing. Two Indians in Wivenhoe! The population had doubled since last week. He was elderly, mid-sixties maybe, in a beige suit with a cream turtle neck and a white silk turban.

'Can you read?' he asked me.

'Yes!' I protested. But maybe his eyes weren't so good any more.

'I mean, do you speak English?'

'Yes,' I said again.

'With all the language schools . . . ,' he explained. 'Now, what are they selling on that stall there, for fifty pence a pound?'

'Sprouts. Brussel sprouts.'

'But what do they call them?'

'Oh!' I laughed, reading the sign, 'Spurts. They've missed

out the 'o'. I like that one there, look, 'obos': aubergines.'

He laughed too.

'Well, I don't know your name,' he said, 'but happy christmas, little stranger.'

'Oh happy christmas,' I said, wishing suddenly that I was wearing my sari. For him I would have worn it. Feminist that I am! He would have liked it, so far from home."

"But why christmas?" asked Averil, "If it meant nothing to either of you?"

"Oh it's not allowed to mean nothing!" Veera exclaimed. "Gurus' birthdays, Diwali, they can mean 'nothing.' But not christian christmas. That's why he said it, a lot safer between us than the other two. With Mrs Gandhi and all."

"Ah," Averil nodded. So that was why Veera spoke English.

"Did you come with Zoe?"

"No, I walked."

"Long way."

"Is that 'long'? I didn't realise. I suppose I wanted a 'long' walk."

"Well you'd better have a drink now," Veera smiled. "I can try out a cocktail on you. When my sister was engaged and her intended was coming to dinner, she would try out every dish the day before on us. Then cook it all again next day."

"Has Kay gone out?"

"She's oaring."

"Rowing?"

"Oaring," Veera repeated, "with Sally."

"That's terrible," pronounced Averil. "The second worst social misdemeanour is to trivialise sex."

"And the first worst?"

"Perverting the course of silence. Talking to avoid saying anything. Mocks both what you say and what you don't. Plus it doesn't work. Because you did say something, didn't you?"

"Yes," said Veera, "but surely half of saying must be that the other woman understands. I don't think you could understand about my sari and the Sikh and christmas."

"Because I'm not Indian? No. But this Women's Studies, then. You are meant to talk about yourselves and you're all different but you will understand?"

124

"Arrogance," said Veera.

"Isn't being a woman binding?"

Veera smiled, "And trivialising sex, then, your second misdemeanour?"

"Sleeping with two women at once."

"Don't men trivialise?"

"Aren't any. Don't stall. Do you want to know or not?"

"Yes."

"Sex is the highest good, the closest you ever get to another being."

"I get it," said Veera, "and silent sex is over the top."

Averil laughed. "Being close to a woman is not being close to others. That's what it means. Look: my hand is close to the black olives because it's further from the green ones. It's comparative. Has to be."

"Otherwise there's just you and black olives for all eternity. What fun."

"Like love," said Averil.

Veera started.

"Not an absolute. In this case: a promise. A statement of intent. 'I intend to be closer to you than to anyone on earth'."

"Isn't this a bit sudden?"

"I love you," said Averil.

"I don't know what you mean."

Kay and Sally were drifting along in a roaring torrent, might any moment be coughed out into the Channel.

"Darling, you were marvellous," said Sally.

Kay shrugged modestly.

"No really. You seemed to suddenly snap out of it when you dragged me up the garden path. The estate agent's face!"

"Too good to pass up," panted Kay, struggling to steer them out of the cross-current.

"He believed you, too. That you'd made an appointment through the other agent."

"Oh they do that all the time," said Kay, "if a house is on several lists and the agents don't coordinate very well, they often end up showing two people round at once."

"Bet they hate that."

"With reason!"

"When you told the young couple about the by-pass, I thought I'd burst.

'Seen a lot of places?'

'This is our first!'

'They begin to blur after a while.'

'Seems very nice. Such a quaint, peaceful village. We love it, don't we, honeybun?'

'It does seem peaceful, doesn't it. At the moment. Sigh. Course, with the new by-pass. . .'

'By-pass?'

'You probably noticed the roadworks as you drove down.'

'Wasn't really looking.'

'Yes, bunny. You remember. You had to start steering again . . .'

'Oh yes.' Giggle.

'All that traffic!'

'Oh you don't mean? No civic conscience. Honestly, they'll ruin the countryside.'

'Well now, anyone any more questions? Any more for any more? Speak now or forever . . . as they say.'

'It's a lovely house.'

'Really lovely.'

'But we thought we ought to see a few more before we settle.'

And they're only building a roundabout! "

Kay basked.

Zoe left the Conversazione as soon as decently possible.

"I've been invited to a student housewarming," she explained, "not my style really, but I don't like to cold-shoulder.

She hailed a cab for Liverpool Street in a great bustle, which lifted once she was safely away. With any luck they were all at Kay and Veera's. She hadn't recognised anyone, peering down from the stage, but then the lights had been on her. The authorities took very little notice, unless someone made them. She was discreet, had an excellent academic reputation, and would not cause anyone to know anything they did not wish.

Zoe had often thought about giving up TWILA, especially after the raid on Gay's The Word, but every month nagging loneliness dragged her to the train and pursued her to London. As she went in and walked across the migraine carpet, she was struck with a sense of this small band, cowering in a basement, even when the place was packed. Lesbians always seemed to get the cellar, or the garret. Once in, however, her spirits would lift with the warm welcome and the drink. They were a good bunch and she would make a special effort to come down mid-week for the literary evening. Tonight they'd had three lesbian writers and a lesbian publisher, which Zoe had agreed to chair. It was very entertaining, and well-attended. All walks of lesbian. In the midst of a wonderful and woefully rare companionship, Zoe had suddenly been wracked with the thought that news of the event might have reached Colchester. Then she simply could not enjoy herself a moment longer, but must get out, out, out as soon as possible. She made her excuses and fled like a child-molester in a blanket bundled out of court.

"You are a bad person and your actions are inexcusable."

"But I'll lose my job."

"Risk it."

"It's not a risk it's a certainty. They seized Jane Rule and *Nice Jewish Girls*."

"How can you have the nerve? If T.he W.ell I.s N.ot L.onely A.nymore it's none of your doing."

"I do about a day and a half a week for TWILA. Unpaid."

"You should get paid for your politics?"

"TWILA's more . . . cultural."

"And your courses?"

"It's up to the students to discuss what interests them. If lesbian students bring up that aspect . . ."

"You don't prevent them? You don't encourage them."

"Well, in my position . . ."

"You don't have to be in your position."

"And I won't be if any of my students were at TWILA tonight."

"Hypocrite! Change from sex to ethics to demonstrate staff responsiveness, then spin round in circles so that no one gets to discuss what really concerns them."

"Not everyone's a lesbian."

127

"Zoe, you make me laugh. You're so pathetic. Work yourself numb for the Department, fill in non-existent moments with TWILA. . . Why don't you give everyone a break and get yourself a lover?"

"Oh I couldn't. They'd all catch on in a minute if they saw me around with Averil."

"Why Averil?"

"She's the only one I'm really interested in."

After a while Zoe tried a different tack.

"You know, education is the state's staunchest supporter, as they say. Funded by money, that type of thing. They are not likely to pay you to undermine them. But you already knew that, didn't you? If they think you're simply picking holes in their social programme, they won't mind. Industry employs problem chasers. If they think you're encouraging their women to neglect them, well. . . That's why you lie low."

Zoe felt very low indeed and longed for the lights of the party. No one, she was sure, could be as hard on her as she was on herself.

The Prow was now sardine-packed. Kay had invited the d.j. from the local women's disco, which meant the disco wasn't on, which meant women on the loose, looking for a place to hang out. At the first bluster of uninvited guests, Veera had felt bemused, recognising them vaguely, thinking that had she known them, probably she would have invited them. As all the rooms in the small house began to fill with smoke, soft piles of outer garments began to encroach upon public throughfares, women spilled out onto The Boards, dancing in freezing darkness, Veera tried to think where she might lie down when the need arose. Friends from along The Boards sympathised and offered their flat as a bolthole; gate crashers filled Veera's glass with champagne, they were celebrating their first six weeks together; someone drove to Colchester for more ice and some pizzas. By the time Kay noticed the house was full of strangers, and had pulled herself together to get rid of them, Veera had already established a non-smoking room, enough ash-trays, more glasses and the general theory that the bedroom was only for coats.

Despite that wealth of opportunity, Kay and Veera, Sally and Averil ended up on the landing together, confirming their warmest assumption, that they were the women they liked best. Cold morning might add that by eleven o'clock, they were practically the only women they knew. And anyway, Averil was stunned by the noise; Veera by the crowd, albeit friendly; Kay was being good and Sally was bitterly disappointed. Zoe, hailed at the door with 'friend of the host or the d.j.?' found herself slowly propelled upstairs with the wriggling inexorability of a loo queue. She levered herself down between Sally and some housewarming cacti, embarrassed to be sitting on the floor, feeling she ought to be wearing beads and a black polo neck. And whatever was she to do with her knees?

"Goodness," she said at last, "what a lot of friends you have."

"Yes," smiled Veera, "we could look at it that way."

"One place I lived," said Sally, "they heard it was a squatters' eviction party. Started tearing down bannisters, wrenching out the plasterboard while the rest of us were making punch. As we were going anyway, they might as well help themselves. Only we weren't due out for another two weeks!"

"Oh Sally," said Kay, "you've really lived."

"They who?" queried Zoe, "The bailiffs?"

"No," Averil explained, "other squatters."

"This is nonsense," Veera announced, summoning her presence, "squatting the landing of our own home."

Kay would have pointed out just who was actually buying the house, but she was on her very best behaviour.

"They've had a good time," Veera continued, "now it's time they went." She did not wish to thread and shove her way down the stairs, into the living room, across to the stereo, fumble for the switch and argue until someone else wearied of turning it on again; instead she opened the little electrical cupboard conveniently positioned by her left elbow, and pulled the bottom fuse. Surprising in one so femme, but Veera understood about fuses. Furthermore she had been made aware, by Zoe's cramped and crumpled figure, that no guest of hers should be required to sit on the floor. Barefoot in India on the lawn with cushions; but in

England no one had feet.

Predictably, downstairs someone screamed and someone else giggled; a glass was smashed and matches were lit. Before chaos, but after confusion, Veera announced that everyone would fill a rubbish bag before they left. She replaced the fuse, handed out bags, and told everyone, guests and gate-crashers alike, how nice it had been, what fun and how kind of them to offer. By the time she bid goodbye to the last one, the house had been swept, glasses washed and pizza scraped off the bathroom floor. Averil stood in the hall matching coats to partygoers with intense accuracy. Sally emptied ashtrays and Kay ferried full rubbish bags to the bins on the sea side of The Boards. Zoe helped herself to a drink and watched everyone depart in noisy, laughing huddles like small boats launched on a dark ocean.

"Onion soup," said Veera, "and then I don't care what the rest of you do, but I am going to my bed."

After the last rubbish bag, and the last coat, the last flurry of missing gloves and crash helmets, the room was bare and hesitant: too much furniture and too few objects. The tailend of a staff meeting. It was the chairs. Too many chairs for a party. And surely, in her day, they'd gone on carousing till dawn. Many a candle had sputtered as the windows were opened on a weak, but promising, sunrise. Zoe removed the single winter crocus from the window sill and put it on the seat of an armchair. Maybe it would fall off. She sat in its place in the wide opening, cut into thick stone. It was all over and she'd only just arrived. Anger and misery. No. No point inviting her simply as a snub. Disappointment, then. Yes. She sipped her brandy and was pleased to discover a naked cigarette stub ground out on the crocus saucer. A fellow oversight. There was even a little stray ash finely littering the top of a bookcase.

"Let's leave the furniture till morning," Kay called down the stairs, 'hello, found your way in here, did you?"

Her tone, although addressing Zoe, was, for once, unaggressive. She dumped her body in a leather armchair and gazed out at the view she had bought. A dark, starry panorama with a sweep of moon, to be replaced by morning and a tidal estuary, mud flats, wooden boathouses, oaks. From an old English family, the oak. Not like the scrubby bushes of Tooting Common where she had strolled with whichever truelove, waiting for rain so the straight teenagers would abandon those same bushes to the queers.

Zoe glanced at Kay from the protective smoothness of her brandy glass. How old was she? Not she, Kay; but she, Zoe. How old was she? Or rather, who were her peers? Women her own age, or women who'd been lesbians all their lives, as she had? Zoe was watching Kay now: those hands, those knees, that back, they'd never bent to please a man, any more than Zoe had. Oh, she'd passed exams, shone at interview, but she'd never yearned for a man's approval, the way Sally dipped and ducked, last knuckle of her little finger curling provocatively into the corner of her mouth. What did Kay see in that? Zoe remembered Veera. Well, yes, Kay was tired of fighting. No, not fighting, losing. Sally was effortlessly inferior.

Something rock solid sat in the armchair opposite Zoe. Whatever they were doing in ten years time, Zoe knew that Kay would be doing it with women. She felt an immense confidence in her, as with the straight dykes at TWILA.

Kay looked up then, felt the warmth and respect curling across the room. Puzzled, she smiled.

Zoe wondered how long Kay had been with Veera, reminding herself to look it up in the college records. She could check their various addresses, or ask Averil, it was the sort of task she might like. Oh, how dreadful. Shame followed immediately upon thought.

"I'm looking forward to the Ethics course next term," Kay was saying.

Zoe was hurt. In her silent musings, she had placed herself and Kay as twin oaks, two lifelong butches, linchpin lesbians. Their imagined conversation started far deeper than college, or even women's studies. Though mere seconds before, Zoe had been planning to snoop.

Kay had not had the row with Veera which must surely be brewing, before they could have sex and sleep secure. They had met, briefly, over the car boot. Kay had hugged Veera, and provoked:

"Is this 'I'm sorry,'; 'I didn't'; or 'goodbye forever'?"

"It's 'Welcome to our new house, darling'."

"And please forget I spent all afternoon with Sally."

"We went to collect the glasses."

"So you said."

Kay, having decided Sally was not worth the risk, wanted Veera to appreciate all she might have lost. She put down the parcels Veera was carrying, and pulled her towards her, kissing her fiercely on the mouth. Veera, who had wanted so much to be reassured in just this way, now felt humiliated, but she let herself be kissed, and hugged Kay tight.

A cessation of hostilities to allow the party to take place. Kay wondered would she be permitted to sleep, or would Veera continue in bed.

"You don't look too sharp, V," Sally was saying, "why don't you rest now and I'll finish off the soup?"

Veera felt too wrecked even to be riled at the nickname, 'V'. Sally led her to a sofa.

"That's better. Strong tea, with lots of sugar and we'll soon have you right."

It was foolish of Veera to let it get this far. She should have lain down hours ago. By now she was swimming dizzily six feet in the air, struggling to stay conscious. She really did not want to faint. She could never quite convince her attendants that losing consciousness was not simply a blank, but extremely painful. They understood dizziness, headaches, nausea, even the terrible fright of disappearing, but she could not seem to explain sufficiently that it was the pain she dreaded worst.

"Oh dear, it's that bad, is it? I didn't realise," said Kay.

"You didn't notice," thought Veera, two feet above her.

Averil appeared with the tea; Sally took it from her and told her to fetch a blanket.

"Meths and brandy," Sally added, "that'll set her up."

Between sipping the brandy and sniffing the meths, having her feet rubbed and being administered sweet tea, Veera began to feel the danger recede.

"I'm so sorry," she apologised lightly, "I have low blood pressure, you see, and it makes me quite confused."

Had she energy left, she would have spent it on anger that she must submit to the ministrations of Kay's newest sweetie. But she only felt how wonderful to have warm toes.

Zoe stood up to offer lifts, Veera's exhaustion scolding her selfishness.

"I do feel better," Veera said, "I would quite like it if you

132

stayed for soup. If you could be calm, and talk softly. It gives me. . ."

Sally and Averil searched for the word for hot soup and quiet weariness. Kay feared it was bad indeed for Veera to tolerate, no request, Sally's continued presence. But Zoe thought of Kay, sitting rock solid in the armchair. It was confidence; that's what lesbians gave you.

". . . confidence," Veera finished.

She did not think she would lose Kay to Sally, though she remained angry that Kay should taunt her with it. When the edge of consciousness brushed close, it impressed Veera with the emptiness of lesbian lives, in constant need of definition and detail. Up there, on the brink of black out, she was even curiously pleased with Sally's curling little finger, cocked, as it was, for Kay.

The low throbbing headache which had dogged the first six months of Averil's new job now eased, as suddenly as the change in programme which clicks the bedsit fridge from pump to hum, and allows you, at last, to think. All her antennae were erect and bristling with the same erotic attention which had first drawn her to Veera as the woman most likely to. . . The same, but concentrated, heightened by five women beginning to close in on the same thought. Averil felt a will to honesty which almost overpowered her with longing. She had begun to think, in her stamp-arranging, letter retyping, Zoe-baiting period, that these women somehow lived without it, that she must adapt her clitoridal truth function to respond to lesser stimuli, or give up on Women's Studies altogether.

"Well," said Sally, "here's soup. Not quite like Veera makes, but it's hot and oniony. And I heated some garlic bread, so you can either dip or crunch." She handed round folded newspaper for under the hot bowls.

"What did I interrupt?" asked Veera, content to leave the bowl on the arm of a chair and let the sweet onion and imperious garlic waft their way to her nostrils, now recovering from the sharp shock of the meths. "You two were quite engrossed when Sally and I blundered in."

The wind rattled and a cold draft forced Zoe out of her window niche and closer to the others. It blew against the wet bushes on Tooting Common, revealing a used durex and a broken syringe.

"Ethics," said Kay, "I was telling Zoe I was looking forward to the course." Kay glanced at Zoe, now seated beside her. "I registered because I wanted a degree, Zoe, and I'm transferring to Statistics next year."

Zoe drew breath.

Kay continued: "It's not such a compromise, though I may give up altogether. But I thought perhaps. . ."

"Me too," said Averil, "I don't want grades and corrections, but I need, at least once a week, to be in a room with a group of women saying something real."

Once a week. Pale shadow. Maybe she could store it up.

"I don't think I could take spectators," Zoe shifted nervously. "The co-ordinator will want progress reports."

"Students are now showing signs of honesty, or at least honourable lesbian intent, for up to five minutes at a time. During next week's lesson I will introduce the concepts of fudging and avoidance. In the first half, we will discover for ourselves the detrimental effects of these widespread practices, and, in the second, we will each say something we mean," laughed Averil.

"You sure we're not practicing to swim the Bay of Bengal underwater?" Sally giggled, with a wink at Veera.

"Maybe we could meet in each other's houses," said Veera. As soon as she had strength enough, her first act of honesty would be the declaration that under no circumstances could she and Sally be in the same group.

The soup was finished, the guests cogitating. When Zoe reached again for her coat and rattled her keys, this time no one stayed her. Sally fell asleep in the back on the way home. Leaving Averil to Zoe.

BE SELECTIVE

"Tell him I'm black," insisted the woman seated before her, "you make sure you tell him I'm a black woman. I'm not going all the way up Enfield to have him tell me the job's taken."

Louie did not know quite what to say. The phone in her hand was ringing; at any moment Mrs Perry would answer it; the black woman was waiting. Louie could have saved them all a wasted phone call. Mrs Perry never took blacks. Why didn't Lou just tell, she peered at the card on her desk, Miss Shirley Etienne, that Mrs Perry would not employ her? Zimmer's had vacancies, perhaps Shirley could try there. Though Zimmer's was tricky. They liked to keep their numbers even, and they only took West Indian blacks.

"We are completely racially integrated," the personnel manager liked to explain to visiting employment officers, "you'll see black and white working happily side by side. We are not prejudiced in the least. We cannot take the Irish, however, because they do not mix with the English, and we cannot take the Nigerians or the Pakistanis because they don't mix with the West Indians."

An ethnic cookery lesson. No, the correct procedure when blacks applied for unsuitable jobs had been clearly outlined by the supervisor. Employers explained confidentially that it was a rather delicate matter. . . and whilst they themselves had nothing whatever against. . . and indeed some of their best friends. . ., and where would London Transport be without. . ., nevertheless their customers wouldn't like it if. . . (the range of tasks delicate customers would not like to see performed by blacks was oceanic: from unblocking their toilet and fixing their drains to machining their coat linings and buttering their ham rolls, customers were most parti-

135

cular). The order clark clucked sympathetically, (The Employer Is Always Right), and jotted BE SELECTIVE in the bottom right-hand corner of the card. She used to write NB, but this was considered at the same time too blunt and too cryptic. A new interviewer might not get it and there was always the possibility of a spot check by RR, though usually they rang to say they were coming. The interviewer was to try simply to put the applicant off. Too young, too old, too far to travel, too big for the uniform. If the applicant proved insistent, you could dial your own home number and let him hear it ring unanswered; or the supervisor's number, and have her say the job was filled. If you got as far as calling the employer's number, often the applicants could be made to give themselves away. A foreign-sounding surname could be made to sound more foreign, or you could hand the receiver over and the applicant's accent would do the trick. Sometimes, despite these careful tripwires, a black person did get to carry a white person's gas oven down the three flights of the old house and up the four flights of the new. This was regrettable.

The phone rang. The black woman waited. Still Lou did not know what to do. It could have been her lover, Colette, in front of her. Lou'd been on the dole nearly three years when she noticed the vacancy. The card was taken down within twenty minutes of being put up, and Lou did not want to lose the job now. Of course they hated blacks, just as they hated Jews, queers and women, but surely if she at least refused unfair treatment, that was one loophole oppressed minorities could crawl through to decent jobs? She tippexed out BE SELECTIVE from the cards when she could, sent women for men's jobs, refused to understand when an employer asked "Is he one of our more suntanned friends?"

But she did not know what to do in the face of Miss Shirley Etienne's quiet persistence. It flashed through her mind that Shirley might be from Race Relations, in which case it was probably better to let her go ahead and see for herself just how white Mrs Perry kept the shopfloor. But RR were wordy and abstract, Shirley was quite direct. If what she wanted was a job, like she said, why feed her to the mangle? Why not look out another card, send her some-

136

where she had a reasonable chance? Now, where was that? As she waited for Mrs Perry to answer, Lou flicked through the cards. Shirley was becoming her personal campaign. She must find her something, show her not all whites were like Mrs Perry.

"What's the matter?" asked Shirley, "Doesn't it answer?"

"No," replied Lou, holding the receiver.

"Praps it's their lunch hour," Shirley suggested.

Lou glimpsed an escape route, but where was there, exactly, to escape to?

"No," she said, "they go twelve to one. Mrs Perry always takes ages. Probly on the other line; she likes to interview everyone herself."

"You know her then?"

It was on the tip of Lou's tongue to say, "She's one of our best employers", as the supervisor did. Perry and Perry's was one of the biggest firms on the trading estate. There was pretty much always a Perry's job on the books. Why didn't Lou tell Shirley, "No black person, man or woman, has been taken on at Perry's since I've been here. That's three months, and they hire and fire every day almost." Because for three months Lou had known of this malpractice and not lifted her little finger.

"I've been up there on an industrial visit," she dodged.

"Tell me straight," said Shirley, "do I stand a chance?"

"Not a prayer," Lou wanted to say, only not enough to actually say it. If Shirley made a complaint, which it was her absolute right to do, and cited Lou as source, Lou would be charged with breaking the Official Secrets Act. What went on between an employer and his employment office, was a matter for him and his conscience. Lou should have spoken to her supervisor, but it was the supervisor who'd come up with all those neat tricks for offloading blacks; then she should have spoken to the manager, but he was married to her supervisor. So she should have told RR. So she should, she should, but they intimidated her with their accents and their college degrees. It was their fault.

Fault located, but no reply had yet been forthcoming. Shirley's question hung unanswered in the air.

"Hallo, Perry and Perry's, Mrs Perry speaking. Who's calling please?"

"Hallo, Mrs Perry, jobshop."

"That's Lou is it? How are you, dear? Hope you've got someone good for me. That Mr Russell you sent up has worked out very well."

"I've a woman here called Shirley Etienne. Post-office trained, good speeds."

"Ettyenne," repeated Mrs Perry, "how do you spell that? Foreign is it?"

Lou spelled it out. "French, I think," she added.

Shirley looked at Lou, "Let me speak to her," she said.

Lou wondered whether to try and intercede. "Praps you'd like to speak to Miss Etienne yourself?"

"Yes, alright," said Mrs Perry busily, "see if she has a good phone manner. Shirley Etienne," she muttered, as if jotting it down, "she is a white woman, isn't she?"

Mrs Perry sounded so sure, that Lou almost said yes. With Shirley sitting quietly across from her, said "Yes, Shirley is a white woman."

"No," said Lou conversationally, "no, no, Miss Etienne is black."

"Don't apologise for me," said Shirley, reaching for the receiver.

"But we don't hire blacks," protested Mrs Perry irritably, "now you know that. Send the girl to Zimmer's."

"Well?" asked Shirley, "What did she say?"

"She says they don't hire blacks," said Lou flatly.

Shirley lifted the receiver out of Lou's hand.

"Mrs Perry? This is Shirley Etienne. I understand you have a vacancy for a clerk receptionist? Well, I'm post-office trained, experienced on most office switchboards, I type eighty words per minute and I can operate a VDU. I'd like to come over this afternoon for a trial."

"Well?" asked Lou.

"She's going to give me a try out," said Shirley, and she picked up her bag to leave.

Well, now she'd blown Mrs Perry's cover. Mrs Perry would have a quiet word in the manager's ear and Lou would be called up for pilfering petty cash, find herself back on the dole bout the same time Shirley got sacked for bad time-keeping. Trumped up, gilt-edged and hermetically sealed.

No. Lou need fear no more than whispers and general mistrust. It suited her idea of equality to believe she and Shirley'd get the same punishment.

Lou decided to call Racists Anonymous, the twenty-four hour line for anyone who fears he might be about to commit racism. They took confession too, though it was rather frowned upon. Backed by weekly support sessions you should become so aware of the problem that you automatically phoned before you did anything. They were thinking of setting up a line for the victims as well, but these things took time and, of course, it depended very much on the success of the first venture.

They'd make her feel better, couldn't do anything with a poor self-image and right now hers was pretty battered. They would examine the particular details of the slight, discuss recent theories of the patterns of prejudice, get her to think back to the first time she became aware of racism around her, of her own racism. And then? Well, she would no longer be smug about it, would be conscious that it was a system which benefitted her, a system she was responsible for maintaining.

She and Colette had been to a local session at the public baths, the inauguration of an awareness training progrmme. Colette said she reckoned black people could be racist same as white. "Well maybe not the same, but if anyone suggested I live in Africa, I'd go spare at the thought." The course elders, (there were no leaders, only more experienced participants, most people who went through one course, signed up for another), advised against Colette's participation. "It gets rather personal," they explained, "nothing wrong with that, have to learn that this means us, but you might not like what you'd hear." Colette didn't like what she was hearing. "I expect there's a black consciousness raising group we could try and put you in touch with." Colette liked this even less.

"So what did you talk about?" she asked Lou as soon as her lover got in the door.

"They said we should remember racism is everywhere, that although its effects are devastating, it's not so big a word we should be afraid of using it. Often it's made up of small everyday acts of humiliation and cruelty. . . ."

139

"Like lynching and slavery?"

Lou cringed momentarily, then steeled herself to duty. "That's what it leads to, sets the atmosphere for. Innocent of enormous crimes, we shouldn't feel exempt from minor prejudice."

"Meaning?"

"Like if you go into an office, thinking the white woman's boss, the black woman's junior."

"You meant to pretend you're deaf, dumb, blind or what? Only I insult deaf, dumb, blind people saying that. When I go into an office, I **know** who's boss, who's junior."

"One of the group's a graphic artist; she was explaining she had to design a poster outlining National Health Services. Before she went through awareness training she would of automatically drawn a white male doctor, a black female nurse."

"Don't say it!" broke in Colette, "Now she draws black women doctors, white male nurses? Sounds like she was more aware before she did the training."

"They reckoned the worst thing was when you started thinking black people are different than white."

"We are."

"Yes, Colette," Lou flinched, "I know that. I'm saying it wrong. They meant that although we have different experiences, we are capable of understanding each other."

"Less and less every minute."

"Don't get angry. I'm just trying to tell you what they said."

"I'm not getting angry. You're making me angry. You stayed there all evening, must have been something keeping you there."

"Okay, so it was mostly a load of rubbish, but not all."

"So give me the good bits, Louie baby, I'm waiting for the good bits."

"When they said racism was a big word but we mustn't be afraid of using it, because it describes even the smallest, meanest negligence. Well that's true isn't it?"

"Maybe," Colette conceded, "only somehow I don't believe it's words white people are afraid of."

"One of the ways racism works is to set black people up as so completely other that they don't even feel what whites

140

know they'd feel in similar situations."

"If you prick us, do we not bleed? If you tickle us, do we not laugh, and if you wrong us do we not revenge?" quoted Colette, "That was nearly four hundred years ago. None of you wasps done any thinking since? What's the matter? Resting on your laurels?"

"Well, of course the situation can't be reversed, it is different, but not unimaginable."

"Why so inarticulate?" said Colette, "If they call a public meeting to start training for something, you're going to be upset if they don't let you in cos of your skin colour, no?"

"Of course!" Lou exclaimed earnestly.

"Yeah, well not when it's racism you're training for."

"But we had to talk about racist things we'd done," Lou protested, "you shouldn't have to listen to that."

"Cept when some white fucker yells it at me in the street? They didn't want me there case I spoiled their fun. Listen, Lou, I don't give a shit about your new found friends, I want to know what you said because you're my lover and maybe we're going to sleep together tonight."

"I told them how I got things duplicated at work," Lou said, trying not to argue with the word 'friend', "the clerical assistant's very friendly with me. I got a hundred copies of the Lesbian Line poster done and she never batted an eyelid. One day I was in there, her mate said Julie, or someone, was back from her holidays. "They say she's as brown as a nigger. Brown as a black, that's what they say." "Yeuch" joked my friend, the duplicator, "tell them to keep her away from me. I can't stand those nignogs near me."

"And what did your wary racists say to that?"

"Not a lot. We were going round in circles blurting things out. You know, like co-counselling where no one listens but they give each other space. Only I got the distinct impression they were angry with me for bringing up the lesbian bit, pleased when the clerical assistant was more racist than homophobic."

The RA line was busy. Just as well. Sympathy was not really what Lou needed. And what did Shirley need? She'd left Lou with no stirring tale of a sick mother, dependent siblings, not even a hefty mortgage repayment. If Lou was going to throw up her job, any chance of re-employment in the area, she could have done with a piteous cause to fight for, stead of routine justice.

A white, middle-aged man sat down in front of Lou. From then till tea break was a steady stream of job seekers, either white, or, if black, applying for appropriate positions. When Toni came to take over, Lou told her she was giving some orders back to the clerk; she thought the numbers had been duplicated. She picked up the pile of BE SELECTIVE cards she had carefully sifted from the drawer. Then she slid their corresponding descriptions down from the display boards.

"Gone already?" asked a black youth who'd been copying out an inappropriate number.

"Too slow, guy," said his mate, "they all 'gone' before we get here."

Lou took her pile into the duplicating room, smiled at the clerical assistant.

"Need some more of these done," she muttered.

After break she went round the filing cabinets to look at the five point plans. No point covering traces. Just had to find what she needed before she was stopped. Otherwise BE SELECTIVE could simply mean 'smart appearance'. Slowly she collected interviews and action details that showed blacks came back saying jobs were taken which, three days later, a white person was sent after. Her heart was throbbing loudly in her chest all the while as she imagined she was robbing a bank vault, but in fact she was there full ten minutes before anyone even asked "What you looking for, Louie? Lost something?"

At five fifteen, Lou left the office, collected her bag from Toni's desk, (couldn't find the key to her own drawer,) shoved the photocopies inside a book, and walked down the corridor. Any moment someone would challenge her; Gill from duplicating would have mentioned her visit; the order clerk would have noticed the cards missing; the manager would ask her to kindly step into his office. She must get the stuff out the building first. Soon the pleasant "Good night, Louie, see you in the morning"s would turn against her, once they knew. Oh, they were only work friendships, and her real life was Colette and the house, but still. She didn't

142

like to think what Colette would say. Lou should have raised hell immediately, before she was implicated; trouble was, by getting the job she'd got herself implicated. Precious few blacks working at the Employment Office either.

Once she and her guilty bundle were safely outside, she wondered what to do with the evidence. Send the whole lot to the papers and they'd do an expose? Which papers? She better write an accompanying letter. Perhaps they'd want to interview her. She couldn't do that. What if they just ignored it? Tore the whole thing up? Must discuss it with someone first, or she'd only get herself into a mess. She'd hoped that nicking the stuff would be the big bit, and now it was only the beginning.

Lou didn't want to do anything that would remind Colette of the differences between them. Sometimes she imagined it welling up like a volcano, splitting the ground beneath their feet, leaving Colette on one side, herself stranded on the other. When she first met Colette, she was obsessed with wanting her. Colette was sharp and honest and Lou felt great need of honesty. She was light-skinned, 'fair' she called herself, (though she laughed at such a white expression,) thin and often silent. Oh the joy in Lou's heart the day silent Colette spoke to her. Each time Lou was answered, Colette ignored, seemed to cut another day off their time together. Colette was being cast out to sea and Lou was being used to push her away. When Colette spoke to black women, Lou saw it as the beginning of an inevitable separation. Colette was quicker and braver than Lou, she at least reached her conclusions without shying away as she saw them coming. Lou liked to discuss things with Colette for that very reason, knowing she did not give the same back. She worried what she did give back and whether Colette would leave her.

When Lou got in, Colette was already home. She asked how it had gone that day, had they found Lou's key or did she still have to keep her bag in Toni's drawer? Lou took a deep breath.

Lou was breathing in, Colette was thinking. Bonnie and Steph usually put her in a bad mood; made her restless, rather. They'd got straight to the point. As always. "You still messing around with that white woman?" It was the 'white' they emphasised; the 'woman' they despised. They knew about white boyfriends, nothing hard to understand in that department. But a woman? Her sisters guessed at Lou's probable faults with near accuracy. They'd had white friends at school. "And however bright she is, she'll turn stupid on you whenever there's something she doesn't want to understand. White woman stupid." "Make that white woman comatose, sister." Except that, Colette feared, Lou wasn't white woman stupid, she was genuinely stupid. At first Colette thought it was just lack of courage; once Lou 'got it', she would fight to the last, she just took her time 'getting it'. Living with a white woman, that was her business, but living with a stupid white woman, that Colette should be ashamed of. Reminded her of fifties role playing. Until Lou got this job at the Employment Office, Colette had gone to work with her briefcase, leaving Lou still warm in bed, and come home to a meal, straight out of the Afro-Caribbean cookbook. Before Lou moved in, Colette'd had one saucepan and one frying pan. When the latter's handle melted over a low flame, Colette simply did all her cooking in the former.

Colette liked Lou's excitability, her graphic imagination. She made funny jokes you wouldn't have suspected her of. The first time they slept together Lou'd said "If you're lying on me now, next time you'll be re-lying on me." Colette supposed she did, really. Lou would have them call Colette out of important meetings, impressing the secretary with her urgency, impossible to leave a message. "Hullo, Bugsy," she would whisper to an incredulous Colette, "I was just checking your cords for old tissues when it hit me how much I want you." See, Colette liked being called 'Bugsy', she liked receiving love calls in the middle of planning meetings, and she wasn't even averse to Lou washing her trousers. But it was a great relief when Lou got herself a job. Though it was still Lou who remembered the light bulbs, Colette who changed them, it was no longer institutional, might simply have been because Colette was taller.

Colette was still thinking. Lou now had sufficient air in her lungs to explain about the jobshop. Which she did, without interruption, for the next half hour. When it was clear Lou had finished, Colette asked,

"Why didn't you object when your supervisor first told you what BE SELECTIVE meant?"

This struck Lou with blinding truth. That was exactly what she should have done. How melodramatic to call the papers, irresponsible not to tackle it herself.

"Yes, but she's not going to explain again for me to protest," said Lou, reasonably.

"Oh for Godsake, Lou. You don't speak only when spoken to? Tell her you won't do it. That you think it's wrong. You do think it's wrong, don't you?"

"Quite the most fiendish thing I ever heard of."

"Then you haven't been listening. If you go straight to the papers, and you find a journalist who's interested, and she accepts these as evidence, and she writes up a scandal, then sure, there'll be an inquiry and people will get sacked. Only to be replaced by other people who'll do the exact same thing."

"What should I say to blacks looking for a job meanwhile? Shall I tell them they got no hope?"

"Lou dear, we know we got no hope. So we live without it. Think black people don't know whether a firm size of Perry and Perry's will take them or not? You could send your stuff to a black paper, maybe The Caribbean Tally, see what they want to do with it. There is a difference between knowing and proving. But see, what's wanted is for this discrimination to stop."

Lou girded herself for a lengthy battle.

And of course the local paper got hold of the story, and got it out before the Caribbean Tally was able to check Lou's information. It was both greatly distorted and greatly played down so that the later report was somewhat disbelieved. Heads rolled, though, and personnel were changed. The order clerk was demoted and Gill the duplicator was dismissed for allowing the machine to be used by an outside agency. The manager stayed right where he was, putting in a good word for the supervisor, his wife. Shirley Etienne was not sacked. She was experienced on most office machinery, post-office trained and she had a nice phone manner. When local firms were being investigated Perry and Perry's was passed over. As Mrs Perry explained, they had not employed many blacks in the past, but Ms Etienne, her receptionist was a godsend and they looked forward to more like her. Lou had worked hard, discussing things with colleagues, urging them, shouting at them. She rang employers to explain the jobshop was no longer prepared to discriminate, why did they think their clients would feel unhappy with a black electrician? Surely in this area half their clients were black. She told black jobseekers what a firm's record was like, adding that if they went for interview she would back them up, checking afterwards whether they got the job, and if not, why not. Colette could not help feeling a certain pride and admiration for Lou, but she wondered why, if Lou could do what needed doing so well now, she had had to come to her for advice.

THE WOMAN WHO LIVES
BY HERSELF

BEWARE

Do you realise there is a rapist loose
in your area? He has already made ten
serious attacks. So far his victims
have been women living alone in base-
ments. He creeps in at the slightest
opportunity: a window left ajar, an
easily picked lock, and lies in wait.
He obviously watches the flat for some
time before pouncing.

As he often wears a mask, we have no
clear description, but some facts have
come to light. He is:

WHITE, AGED 20-50, MEDIUM BUILD, WITH
BROWN HAIR. SPEAKS WITH A LONDON ACCENT.

ACTION

1. ASK YOUR CRIME PREVENTION OFFICER –
PC CONRAD COURT, TO CHECK THE SAFETY OF
YOUR HOME.

2. WHEN YOU OR YOUR NEIGHBOURS SEE A MAN
ACTING SUSPICIOUSLY, REPORT IT TO THE
POLICE.

3. KEEP YOUR CURTAINS CLOSED AND YOUR
FLAT BRIGHTLY LIT.

4. COME TO THE PUBLIC MEETING ON THURS-
DAY. (women only.)

Tessa Silverman
93a Dorcas Terrace
London W.11
25/10/83

Dear Sisters,

You make him sound like an escaped lion. Are not all women aware, always, that there is a rapist in their area, if not in their homes, and if not one, several? This one 'creeps in' to basement flats, others head for the open park, pick off lone joggers, cyclists, or they keep it in the family so it's easier to do, more difficult to denounce. And if we are not aware, are not the papers there every morning to tell us? Or our fathers or our husbands, by which I mean any man: shopkeeper, workmate, boss who stands in custodial relation and can therefore expect some little womanly service: a smile, a meal, a thigh.

But what I wanted to tell you, (and I cannot make the public meeting), is how much I enjoy living by myself. For ten years I did the shopping by rota, with a list; cooked ugly substantial meals with the correct protein/carbohydrate balance every nine days; prodded my housemates for their rent and their troubles since either would pile up if left, and cascade. I was, and I quote, "a drain-like sympathetic ear down which one could pour out one's heart's thoughts, knowing they would not get clogged up in the grid of judgement." Now I live in this spacious, sunlit, Notting Hill basement (hence the 'a' of my address). I dine almost exclusively off crumpets with Lurpak and mature English cheddar or black cherry jam which I buy as often as I pass

149

the deli; and I limit my drain-like qualities to the occasional crying friend met unexpectedly in the street and calmed down in a cafe with a cup of tea I didn't have to make. I planned to eat out every night, somewhere obscure and cheap, like Simone de Beauvoir. But, alas, there is neither the climate nor the money. Sometimes, still, I find an odd, withered courgette in my fridge, bought in memory of a time when fridges needed courgettes, never mind did any of us like them. I do not yet know all the things I like, but each fresh button mushroom, each soft toilet tissue is a delight and a wonder. Slowly I am buying things to fill this flat: a fourth mug, a colander, a calor gas heater, and all the worry of it, the price of it, is mine. I am a householder, a grown up; my ear is no longer mutely sympathetic, nor my judgement clogged.

But what I wanted to say (for I'm busy Thursday night), is how frightened I am at living by myself. I have had to furnish the flat, you see, get the drains done, the phone connected, the gas refilled. And every time the delivery man asks:

"Which one is your bedroom? Thanks for the tea."

Or the plumber:

"You the only one using this? Two sugars please."

Or the engineer:

"You in during the day? Drop more milk, ta."

I wonder, "Is this him? Is he looking for a window slightly ajar, a door with an easy lock? Wants to know my movements, easier than watching for hours."

"How long will this bottle last?"

"Can't say, love. How often are you in? Do you sit in this room? My name's Larry, thanks for the tea."

Is it more likely to be him, because he knows me? Or less, because I know him? Than all the other white, medium built, twenty to fifty year olds who walk into me on tube platforms, whistle at me in pubs, hit me through car windows, whom I learn to fear generically, if not individually, simply because they are men, and my fear is useful to them. I have not been raped, or forced to have sex (except by a boyfriend, and that seemed at the time different). I have been pulled into a dark narrow street, pushed up against a wall, had my breasts squeezed and my cunt grabbed (and afterwards invited home for coffee). My house has been broken into by men who, had they not been intercepted, would, I believe, have raped me. I have been assaulted, abused, spat at. As have we all. And I have had nightmares.

I dreamed I came home late at night and very tired. I left my bike outside while I unlocked the front door and, with the door wide open, walked slowly through every room of my flat, looking into cupboards, behind curtains, turning on all the lights. I do this every night, even when I am awake, and I can never decide: should I leave the front door open, in case I need to get out, or closed, in case someone has followed me? Tonight, in the dream, everything was as it should be. I brought my bike in and double locked the door. Then I went into my bedroom, which is cavernously big, running the whole width of the front, with windows onto the street. I walked heavily towards the bed, exhausted, wanting only to sleep, dreamless and inert, but kicked against something on the floor which I realised, on looking down, was a large, black crow with a broken wing, croaking and cawing in hopeless circles. I am too tired to take care of the bird. Either it will be dead by morning, or I will see to it then. I fall leadenly asleep. Suddenly in the night, in the dream, I wake up. It has dawned on me horribly about the bird. If it found a way in, who else did? I think of the woman in the Guardian, coincidentally also called Tessa, who awoke from her sleeping pills to find she had already been raped (though she had no memory of that) and a man was lying on top of her. I get up with a jerk, unable to lie quiet a moment longer, and there, on the carpet, the crow is cawing and turning its irregular circle. I go over to bandage and soothe it, but it is too late. It lifts its long wing over its head, and, in the motion, becomes the man it always was, wearing a black raincoat, his face horribly-scarred and therefore masked. He flies at me. I run through to the back garden. And scream for the women upstairs. Who don't look out.

And at that point I woke up, but unlike dreams of falling,

of public humiliation, of being chased by vampires, I could not, on opening my eyes, tell myself it was all just a nightmare and go back to sleep, for I woke up in that cavernous bedroom with its windows onto the street. Though there was no crow croaking on the floor, still this was a basement in Notting Hill where a man had raped four other women already. I got dressed, fully, including pants and socks. I checked all the rooms again, all the windows, both doors. I made a cup of tea, and sat with all the lights on, and I knew I couldn't stay there.

I would go to Belinda's, that was sensible, she's only round the corner. Or Stella's, or Mandy's or Heather's. I know a lot of women round here. Then I looked at the clock. It was three thirty in the morning. Someone would have to get out of bed, scared as me, and this was only a nightmare. How often would I have to leave my flat in the middle of the night? Half the week I manage to stay at my lover's, through a mixture of half-truths and cunning. "It's so much more comfortable here." "You've got central heating." "I've run out of olive oil." I am a grown woman and I hide my fear behind olive oil.

If you wake early one morning to find a round orange slug curled under your table, don't be alarmed, it is not me crouched terrified in my sleeping bag; it is surely a very rare and delicate snail. It might even be good to eat.

You want to send a police officer Conrad over to check that my home is safe. Like the plumber checked the drains? Like the engineer checked the phone wires? Before I moved in I spent thirty pounds on locks. They say four rapes in a year is not unusual for a population of this size. There will not be a noticeable bulge in the crime figures.

I came home from work one day to find the door to the electric cupboard ajar. It's damp in there, I always keep it shut. Someone had been in the flat. In the kitchen the window was broken, large pieces of glass on the floor, streaks of blood on the sofa. Drawers upturned on the carpet. My shirt, lying on the back of a chair, newly ironed, was covered in splatters of blood. A little trail of bloody fingerprints led from kitchen to living room to bathroom, ending in my bedroom. The top of the dresser was studded with round, shallow holes: wider than a high heel, too deep for a burn. Of course. A hammer. Whatever he had used to break the window. I shivered. On the table a jewellery box spilled out: nothing missing but a pearl ring and a diamond ring I had not been able to sell. Thank heavens he'd found something. Otherwise would he be waiting for me now, hammer in hand? I did not call the cops. Not even my crime prevention officer Conrad. The blood and fingerprints would have been very useful to them. I wrapped the bits of glass in newspaper, replaced the old pane; scrubbed out my shirt, hung it on the line. I did not want to tell the police there was a vulnerable woman living at number 93a. A lesbian. Fair game. Unprotected by other men.

Now it is four o'clock in the morning. I have written this letter to you and feel better. I have left my bed made, so it looks like no one has slept in it, and moved the cushions from that cavernous front room into my tiny study at the back. I have folded my duvet in half, and slipped my body in between. The telephone is by my pillow; the emergency cord, to the women upstairs, hangs at the foot of the cushions. Though I may not sleep comfortably under your table, at least I can curl up under my own. Behind the door is a wooden chair, under my pillow a hammer. When the man comes, after he has padded through my flat, not finding me in the bed where his calculations led him to believe I slept, just as he is leaving, his purpose unfulfilled, opening this, last and smallest door, with casual curiosity, expecting brooms, pops his head round, having missed the light switch, I, standing on the chair, shall smash my hammer down so hard on his skull that his brown hair will grow matted with his blood, the very bone will crack, his brain will ooze and never again will his tongue speak with a London accent.

Soon I will go back to sleep and tomorrow I will buy myself a hot water bottle, padded with blue Chinese silk, all

I now lack for my comfort. I suggest you stock up, I can let you know where to get them; push them through the letter box while you're giving out the hammers. So much more hopeful than a leaflet telling us to be frightened. Some of us are very good at that already.

In sisterhood,

Tessa Silverman

THE ARCHIVIST

One

Frances lay quite still on the daybed and gazed at the birds pecking the nuts she had hung for them. Every now and then they crashed into the window and their beaks rang out against the glass and the silence. It was sunny. Her living room always seemed to be full of sunshine. It followed her round the room, from the wheelchair to the kitchen, couldn't get away from it. And the central heating going full blast. She had the home help refill those two cups every day and they were always empty. Meant to compensate for the radiators. So stuffy. Sucked all the moisture out. But Ada filled up the cups again and it went on. On and on. Good old Ada. Oh where would we be without the like of Ada?

If she hadn't taken that terrible fall, and it could have been worse, Dr Hanson said, could have broken every bone in her body, stead of crushing a few miserable vertebrae. Out with a bang. If she hadn't taken that fall, Frances would have liked to have been a home help. Well a companion, perhaps. More fitting. Receive the squirming, helpless gratitude she had to give to Ada.

Really it was too unfair. Ada was barely literate, couldn't even read the labels, had to ask in the shop. And she smelt. Couldn't fault her for kindness, kindest creature on two legs, but one wished she would wash in between.

What was that? Oh dear, not the fire alarm again. No peace in this place anymore. Not even peace. Oh, the telephone. Frances dragged herself slowly up by sliding her elbows along the daybed and levering her back into an upright position. If she could only managed to bypass that one bend in her spine, it wouldn't hurt so much. There. Oh, missed! Oh damn it! Damn it all, how it hurt. Oh God, oh misery such pain.

"Hullo, hullo, is that Granny Frances?"

Yes it was Granny Frances. And who the hell else could it be? Did Alison imagine she might have slipped off somewhere out of ear shot?

"Granny, it's Alison. I'll be down on Sunday so you can tell Ada. It is Thursdays, isn't it, for the shopping?"

"Yes, yes, Thursdays. Oh dear. That's better. Well, what would you like to eat?"

"Oh whatever."

"I don't eat much myself, so I've no idea."

Really it was too bad to have to think up menus at her age. At least the boys would say, then she could send Ada out for it, after explaining to the poor woman exactly what it was. But Alison was so retiring. Or bloody-minded. Or . . . Frances could not think what it was quite, about Alison. The boys would never bother to phone and remind her they were coming, simply expected her to be there with chocolate fudge cake, jokes and stories as she'd always been. They didn't seem to notice how she had crumpled and shrunk. It was easier with them, she knew what they wanted: a good meal, a small valuable trinket to take home in their pockets and whatever she could say about them: winning stories about their childhoods, clever little Bobby, clever little Dominic. That's what she was for them, a personal archives. And Alison grated on her, like the grating together of her two lowest vertebrae. It was a vicious comparison.

"Anyway, how are you, Granny?"

"Dreadful. Oh dreadful. Very bad."

"Oh dear, your back?"

"Yes. And I've wrenched my side. I slipped you see. Last week it was. Managed to cling onto the curtains to break my fall but I've pulled all the muscles what with gripping so hard."

"Sounds ghastly."

"It's terrible. Keeps me awake. I phoned Dr Hanson last week but he wouldn't come. Said it sounded like I'd strained something and there was nothing he could do."

"Oh! He should still have come. Imagine not coming! At least he could reassure you it wasn't anything worse. How can he know that without seeing you?"

"Old women are meant to hurt, teach them to live too long."

"You do sound low."

"It's all such a worry. And now this fire."

"What fire, Granny?"

"Oh yes. We had a fire."

"What in the home? I mean in one of the flats?"

"Yes, my dear, completely gutted. And do you know they didn't come for me? I was the only one. They got everyone else downstairs, herded them into the hall, but I could have been burnt in my bed. And I told the police as much."

"What?"

"Yes. Burnt alive."

"Did they forget you?"

"Forget? Forget me? Don't be silly. I think she was trying to kill me."

"But why, Granny, and who? Who is this woman?"

"Well I'll tell you the whole story on Sunday. But I have to move you know, really, I can't stay here."

Did Granny Frances think she was one of the boys, who had to be enticed down to Kent with the promise of a murder story?

Two

Frances was in the kitchen spreading a tea cloth over the tray of knives and forks when Alison arrived.

"Hallo, Granny, it's me," Alison called from the little hallway.

Frances turned slowly, leaning on her cane. Of course it was Alison. It was Sunday. Had she a whole herd of stray visitors to pop in? "Cooee, we were just passing." Didn't she keep a careful record of which grandchild came when, so that she knew how soon she could again extract a promise of a visit? "Bobby, dearest boy, I haven't seen you for such a long time, three months it must be." "Oh not as long as that, Granny, you do exaggerate." "Yes," Frances would repeat

157

firmly, "three months to the day."

"Well," said Alison, stepping into the kitchen, still in her luminous cyclewear, "how nice to see you on your feet."

"Alison, my dear child, how good of you to come."

Kiss, kiss. Peck, peck. Powdered skin to wind-bitten cheek.

"But you're frozen. Help yourself to some sherry, it's on the card table next door. And my goodness me, what are you wearing? Turn around, my dear, turn around."

"It's for the bike, Granny."

"You look like a green luminous frog. Did anyone see you come up here? Don't suppose they could have missed you in that rig out. The warden, did she see you? Did you speak to her?"

"Didn't see anyone, Granny, just parked my bike and came on up."

"Where? Where did you leave it? You're not allowed to put it in the hall. They don't let you. No bicycles in the passageway. Mrs Riggs won't like it."

"I'm sorry. I didn't know. I'll go and move it."

"No don't bother. Not now. I have such a lot to tell you and I'll need your advice. It's been awful."

Frances lowered herself carefully onto the daybed.

"Pass me that shawl, there's a good girl."

"Here you are. Can I make you a hot water bottle? Oh and would you like a drink? I'll refill your glass."

"Me? No, never touch the stuff. Can't. Doctor's orders."

From the lefthand corner of Frances' mouth and away down towards her chin was a distinct dark stain; it stood out red, sherry coloured against the dry powder of her cheeks. Now that the cataract had taken the sight from her right eye, it might have been difficult for her to see it. Not so Alison.

"Oh dear. There. Get the wreck on the deck. Hideous creature. Well now, this fire. Do you know we had the police round? Took a statement. I had simply no idea, thought it was all routine. Then there was this in the papers."

Frances patted the tray with her fingers until she found what she wanted. With her sight failing, she had to lay her memory out in front of her. She passed a folded newspaper to Alison.

DEPUTY WARDEN GRANTED BAIL

Mrs Janice Simmonds was granted bail of £500 at Marfield County Court today and ordered to appear again in 10 days time to answer charges of arson. She is accused of causing a fire which completely gutted a flat in St. Stephen's Resthome, endangering the life of one of the residents, the Honourable Frances Miles-Whitaker. . .

"Good Lord," thought Alison, "so Granny's an Honourable now is she? One never knows."

The Miles hyphen she was used to. Frances used her husband's name and what easier slip than a dash between first and surname?

"Don't you think they should have told me I was making a statement? I mean, she did it alright, but one likes to be careful. Complete psychopath. Is that what they call them? There was that series of false alerts, just after we were wired into the police station. You know, I think she held her cigarette up to the alarm and the smoke set it off. But that wasn't enough for her. Had to have a real fire, with real danger. Not enough excitement in her life. Well, I suppose it isn't very exciting looking after a bunch of old women who have only one more thing to do in their lives and that is to die."

Frances twisted a moment on her cushions.

Alison wondered with sudden horror whether her grandmother could possibly have wheeled herself down to the ground floor, broken into the empty flat and set it alight, when she remembered Frances' fingers in the tray groping for the newspaper cutting. Could the deputy warden be convicted on Frances' evidence alone? Surely not.

"What do you think?" asked Frances.

"Me? I don't know. Were you the only one to give evidence?"

"Well I didn't know it was evidence, did I? But it seems I'm the only one to speak out here. Anyway, lets change the subject, morbid topic. I'm glad the warden didn't see you. She's on Mrs Simmons side. They want to move me downstairs into a tiny little room with no birds at the window, and I keep telling them there's no earthly point because I'll be leaving soon."

"And will you?"

"Well, my dear, that's what I want to talk to you about."

Although quite used to being wary with her grandmother, Alison felt like she'd been on red alert ever since she walked in the door. She wondered whether she'd last out, guard raised, till her Granny's purpose became clear.

"Now let's eat. We can talk business later."

Alison went through to the kitchen and filled a tray with chicken and salad. There were empty plastic bags drying out on every possibility from the taps to the milk bottles. Frances stored all her rubbish in bags before committing it to the bin so that Ted, the neighbour who emptied it for her, should not be assailed in his task by unpleasant odour.

"Here you are."

Alison helped Frances into the wheelchair where she ate, flicking up one of the pedals so the old woman could clamber in, remembering to put the brakes on so the chair did not jerk as Frances sat down. She fitted the tray to the chair and filled the plate.

"I won't eat all of that."

"Try. You can always leave it."

"But such a waste when I know I don't want it."

Alison put a little porcelain bowl of water beside the plate for Frances to clean her teeth in when she'd finished. They ate a while in silence. Alison was glad of the chance to smooth out her stomach knots before it was time to clench them again.

"Well," said Frances softly, fumbling towards something from her wheelchair, "I wonder what my enemy has to say to me." She opened the glass cover of the clock by her daybed and patted the hands wih her forefinger. "Time, my enemy, my old enemy," she murmured, "what are you telling me now?"

"It's ten past one," said Alison factually.

Frances grimaced.

"Well now," she said, recovering herself, "how are you all in London? Dominic says he scarcely ever sees you, what with the life you lead."

Alison didn't rise to it. "I rang Bobby the other day, he

160

was fine. Busy with his poly and his politics."

"Hmph, Bobby. Of course he never comes. Though I hear his Lindy's doing well with her singing. Practices in a proper studio. I expect Bobby can afford it. Do you know he makes poor Dominic pay £25 a week for his room. Isn't it shocking? His own brother."

Alison swallowed hard. "She sings well, Lindy. Lovely voice."

"Always so quiet and timid when she comes here with Bobby. Not that I've seen them recently."

"Oh she belts 'em out. Good dress sense too. Bright colours. Lots of silver. Slinky, jazz type."

"She's good is she? Well that's a relief. Tell me, does she wear a G-string as well?"

Sweet Jesus Granma, you're laying it on a bit thick.

"No. I didn't mean that. I must have given you the wrong impression."

"Pity about her hair."

"Her what?"

"Well she doesn't keep it clean. Just lets it hang there in front of her face."

"I think she has lovely hair. So long and thick."

"Yes well, you have your own ideas about feminine beauty. No, she isn't very clean. And the way she keeps the house, no idea. Do you know I went there when your poor father was so ill, dying he was, and the place was filthy. My poor son living in that squalor, dying in that squalor. I don't like to think of it. Dishes piling up in the sink, everything so dusty, and no clean towel in the bathroom. She could have washed the sheets for him. There are laundry places these days, aren't there, coin-in-the-slot. Couldn't cut his own toe nails, can you imagine?"

Alison could imagine, could remember it all too well to do anything but change the subject clumsily.

"Is that a new photo of Bridey, Granny?"

Frances peered.

"Yes. She doesn't forget her old granny. Always sending me cards and snapshots, little sweetheart."

"Not so little. She was taller than me when I last went out."

"Poor mite. Course she's grown up Canadian now. Expect

161

she has one of those dreadful twangs. Eight years old when your mother did her bunk. Tell me, why did Magda leave your father? Was it because he was so ill?"

"I don't know, Granny," Alison managed, "I was sixteen. Do you think she'd have told me?"

The room was alive with old family dramas. Magda leaving for Canada, taking little Bridey with her. Alison's father trying to explain it all to his daughter, who already knew and had helped plan the escape. "It's her age, you know, they call it the change of life. Perhaps it's better if she does go away for a bit. You've probably noticed how odd she's been lately, that's nervous depression," he paused. "We all have to help each other now." Her father sat on Alison's bed, folding the sheets with his hand, "You do love me, don't you?" Sudden terror in his eyes, suddenly turned beseechingly towards her. Alison, dutiful daughter. "Yes, Daddy, of course." Never went back till the day the nurse phoned. "Now don't worry. Your father's in hospital. Perhaps you'd like to see him." A bunch of orange tulips dropped numbly onto the nurses' table as Alison tried hopelessly to phone Bobby, tell him their father was dead. "Oh God don't let them make me look at him. I don't want to look at him." What happened to the tulips? Were they put in water and handed out to some more deserving patient? Tulips. Pathetic even as a gesture. Alison dare not dwell too long on them or she would cry and Granny Frances would win. Quite what was unclear, but tears were unquestionably a match point. Bobby had married Lindy quickly, when they were both only seventeen, because his big sister had moved out and he didn't want to look after his father on his own. And at seventeen and still a school girl, Lindy was to cut her father-in-law's toenails? All of it, all there in her Granny's snug little living room with the birds pecking at the nuts outside, the accumulated bitterness of the years behind every silver framed photograph. Frances believed in female sacrifice.

"Oh," said Frances, "I was forgetting. I have something for you."

Again her fingers groped in the tray.

"Here you are, dear, I thought you might know something about this."

Alison unfolded the paper.

GERMAINE GREER FACES THE PRESS

"... and on lesbian involvement in the women's movement Ms Greer was equally germain: 'Every progressive movement has its parasites. Even the Colorado beetle carries its dung around with it.'"

Granny Frances with her pain and her cataract, her magnifying glass with its special directional light, had searched slowly and excruciatingly through all the papers till she found something unpleasant about lesbians, 'the dung of the women's movement', and then she had cut round it with her sharp scissors and her acheing hands. Stab. Her trump card. But what, oh what, was the game?

"Well. What do you make of that?"

"Don't know really. I suppose she was trying to sell books. What was it you wanted to talk to me about?"

"Let me see. There was that clipping I thought you might like, now I've shown you that. Oh yes, the fire. Well dear, it's a terrible thought that there might be a fire in the building and I wouldn't be able to get downstairs."

At last she would talk about it without throwing in a murder plot to ensure a hearing.

"But you'd pull the emergency cord and someone would come."

"Ah but I might not wake up. I take pain killers you see, and sleepers, five or six a night, the doctor knows. I think that's why I didn't hear the alarm go off."

"They should still have come for you," Alison protested stoutly to reassure her grandmother, who looked as though she had just let slip a terrible secret.

"I want to move now. Well I don't want to a bit. I've lived all my life in Kent, but I do really have to. Not into a council place. I couldn't bear a dormitory, never shared with any one but your grandfather, and a nursing home would be beyond my means, I'm afraid. I was thinking of a room in someone's house, a downstairs room wih a bathroom on the ground floor. I could afford about £70 a week. Now someone might be glad of that, only have to make my meals and pop in once in a while to say hello how are you. Ada does two hours a day, so that's company, but I'm all on my own for the other twenty two and it's not fun, it really isn't. I can't read with my eye the way it is, and the television's just a blur. One gets to thinking the most morbid thoughts. Do you know of anywhere like that? Someone with an empty room. In the outskirts of London, Dulwich or Richmond perhaps, so I could be near all of you."

So that was what Frances wanted. How slow of Alison. She wanted Dominic's room at Bobby's as soon as Dom moved out. She must have persuaded Dominic it was too expensive for him. Difficult to organise though, if Bobby's visits were erratic, and surely Frances knew that the real fight would be with Lindy, whose lot it would be to look after her? Alison did not see why Lindy should be put through it again, even to the guilt and misery of having to say no. What was to be done? Frances was vicious, but she was old and ill, and could not live by herself much longer. Perhaps it would be possible to find a small home for the elderly, run by someone old enough herself not to be swamped by Frances. Of course, what Alison was meant to do was to try all other resources and fail, then her Granny would have to move to Bobby's, because there wouldn't be anywhere else.

"Well, do you?"

"I might," said Alison finally, wondering would Greta have a list of licensed homes. "A lot of councils allow ex nurses and people to run places, they subsidize the cost and keep a check on what goes on."

"Oh," said Frances, "I expect it'd be a terrible bother to you, would it? Though I'd have moved heaven and earth for any of you when you were small and vulnerable."

It wasn't true. The boys, certainly, Frances had put herself out for, but not Alison. It meant so much more to her to have something she could give a man. Money, sex, information, comfort. Frances felt somehow raised herself by the sex of her recipient.

"I'll see what I can do," said Alison.

She'd be as good as her word. Did her granny know that, used as she was to the pretty caprices of the boys?

"Thank you," said Frances. Cold as always to her grand daughter.

164

Or so it seemed to Alison. "I'm afraid I have to be going now," she said, "my train's at six ten and I have to ride to the station."

"Well it's been wonderful to see you. I so look forward to your visits. All of you. Could you refill this bottle before you go? It's the distilled in the door of the fridge. Oh, and wedge the curtains behind that vase, otherwise they trail in the cups of water on the radiator."

Alison always announced her departure three quarters of an hour before she really had to leave, to allow Frances time to get used to the idea, and avoid last minute urgency.

"I'll refill your hottie, shall I? I'm sure that one's cold by now."

"Do. And would you tape up the side of that tea cloth on the kitchen wall? Your brother Dominic gave it to me and I can't quite reach. Isn't it spendid? That's his ship, you know, the Discovery, the one he's renovating."

There was now only the half hour left before the train, which Alison needed to cycle to the station. Once more clad in her luminous green cycle wear, she braced herself for a last peck on Frances' cheek, before she would be released into the soothing chill of the February air. Oh the promised relief. Already she could feel herself relaxing.

"Bye, bye now Granny. Look after yourself. Shall I leave this door open or shut for you?"

"Open, open. And the hall door shut. Goodbye, my dear, goodbye. So nice. Lovely to see you. Time has flown. Do you know your great grandfather, my father, was a hundred and four when he died? Amazing to think of. Though I hope I shan't have to serve anything like as long. Too awful to contemplate. He didn't look so bad on it. There's a photo of him on his hundredth birthday. It's in the drawer to your right, do you see it?"

Alison rummaged roughly in the little pearl cabinet. She had to go. She'd miss her train and arrive too late to go to Greta's. Lordsakes, she'd given her granny nearly an hour's warning. And she'd said she'd find a home for her. Well she would. Bout time these lesbian social workers did something for their own.

"I can't find it, Granny, I'm sorry. And I've really got to . . . Oh, this must be it. Here you are. But what's this? 'My

Cornish Direy' by Alison Whitaker."

"Oh my, is that in there too? Well you might as well take that with you, though I want it back. You sent it to me when you were nine, after your holiday in Cornwall. You wanted me to imagine you there because I couldn't come."

"My God, I remember! What a surprise. Hey, listen to this: 'Bobby was given a fishing line today. Daddy offered to fix the parts together, so he and another man did. When they were going to put the line on, they found it was all tangled up. So Mummy started to untangle it, but she found it was too muddled. So in the end Bobby had to buy a new line."

Frances nodded and laughed. "Such dexterity! My favourite is the bit about the frogs."

"What's that? I don't remember."

"About three pages further on."

"Hmm, lets see. Oh yes, here we are. 'At night when I was in bed Mummy woke me, and told me to come outside. I did so but could not see anything at all unusual, until I was shown. It was frogs. Lots and lots of frogs, all croaking together'."

Alison snorted. "I remember that croak! Nowp, it went, nowp, nowp."

"Nowp!" said Frances croaking from the daybed.

"Nowp!" Alison answered her.

"That's you," said Frances, "in all your bicycle get up. A luminous green frog."

Briefly, Alison turned to smile at her.

Three

Alison cycled madly past the misty Kent fields, the cold crisp and cutting against her ears.

"She kept it!" the thought sang as she pedalled, "All these years my granny kept my Cornish Direy."

She tugged her sleeve back hurriedly from her left wrist to look at her watch. It was five to six. Another five miles to go. Twenty miles an hour. Well, it was possible.

"She even knew what page the frogs were on!"

Alison sped on through the darkness. Now the long stretch between Biddenden and Headcorn; if she could reach the dairy before five past, she'd make the train. Car headlights loomed up behind and roared past, grew gigantic and dazzling in front of her. "Dip them, goddamn you," she swore as she swerved up a low bank and down again into the road, "can't pretend you didn't see me in my frog suit."

The lights of Headcorn up ahead. Her lungs already spluttering, calves acheing, Alison shot into the station yard just as the train was pulling in. She threw the bike over her right shoulder, raced up the steps, and down onto the London platform. The door of the guards' van was swung open, Alison thrust the bike inside and as she scribbled out a label, she thought,

"And I'll tell you something else. When I was nine years old I wrote down all the interesting things that happened each day for my Granny Frances, because she couldn't come to Cornwall and I wanted her to imagine me there. There was a time when I loved that old woman. And she remembers it too."

Four

Frances lay quite still on her daybed and gazed at the drawer which Alison, in her haste, had left open. So, after all, she was to Alison the same as she was to the boys. An Archive. But at least Alison had the foresight to make the deposit herself. The boys depended entirely on their grandmother's failing memory. Frances hoped Alison would not forget her promise. She would prefer to die in the house of one of her relatives, but she could see there would be difficulties and really, she was too old for them. A clean room with a window over a garden, and some birds, and Frances would die happy enough. Now she was tired. It was so exhausting, making people do right by you. Perhaps she would sleep tonight without pills, that would be nice, and maybe she would dream again, warm colourful things from before she smashed her spine.

THE SAD FACT

Part One

Boyd flew in great swoops across the city, diving down only to shoot back up, up. On she swept over Chelsea Bridge with its vaseline lights and swaying rain. Sometimes she hovered, belly to the road, to feel the tar print roughness on her gliding tyres. Round Sloane Square at a speed that spun her over, almost horizontal. Too quick for the human eye, she could pass through any wall of metal of black taxi cab; out the other side before its molecules could combine, or collide, with hers.

Eight vodkas the steadier, she was going to see Candida. At that hour of the night she was invincible, irresistible. Candida would not resist her.

This superb creature had the grace and delicacy to dodge droplets of fleeting rain and arrive dry and mighty for her lover-to-be. She was as tall as a ceiling and swifter than any phone call. Her forearms strained the fabric of her shirt sleeves; her fingers, capable of the softest glide, were too wide to dial a phone number. Her eyes, even in the dark, were blue and pale; so pale they were not eyes at all but light itself. Pale blue beams of intense concentration. Her nose was long and slightly crooked; whoever broke it was clearly the sadder and wiser for it. Her mouth was large and her lips were sloppy, as ripe mangoes are sloppy, tight with the rip of teeth and the wetness of flesh.

All unknowing, Candida dripped wet footprints from the bath to the bedroom. She had forgotten the American towel drying on the radiator. She rubbed the now cooling damp off back and breast and huddled into a flannel nightie. To procure a hot water bottle she would have to descend to the kitchen and each step would jolt her precarious and seething head. Candida had a migraine.

Part Two

Candida savoured a guilty mouthful of fresh parmesan before grating a lump over the farfalle. She had ground pinenuts by hand, plucked basil from her own hot-housed plant. As she raised her fork, she caught a whiff of something missing. Here was food, and hunger, and time to savour both, but: no praise. No one but fellow cooks, whose number were few and voices jealous, realised what a marvel was the food they were eating. But Candida set a standard: perfection, whose absence was quickly detected, by even the most wolfing palate, when the same dish was served elsewhere.

Candida would like to have given the world pesto sauce. She would like to have fed Boyd. So that next time Boyd ate in the canteen she would tell her workmate, 'Mine's an omelette. Their pasta doesn't taste right.'

The meal eaten, the chopping boards rinsed, Candida drifted upstairs. She bathed in brimming tea rose, sure that Boyd was, even now, on her way, though the last tube had gone and no word had been spoken. Boyd would be hungry for nothing but Candida.

Candida crested the wave to turn off the hot; the incessant dripping was boring small holes in her skull. Tighter and tighter she turned, harder and harder she gripped, but the drip widened in a ripple, spreading viciously. Candida had a migraine. Either she must toss and groan the night away, or Boyd must ring the bell within the next five minutes. Only sex before it reached the cerebellum could shake the headache off.

All unknowing, Boyd coasted to the front door, slick with sweat and panting. She gazed upwards to the unlit windows of Candida's sitting room. Ghostly grey daffodils fingered the breeze. Candida would be curled asleep around a hot water bottle. Her keys unfixed to any tennis ball to be thrown like a ladder of hair from a tower window, Candida must descend four flights. Boyd passionate, was not cruel; mistook her previous confidence for presumption, turned sadly from the doorbell.

Part Three

Boyd shouldered open the plastic doors of St Bart's. One of her brother's blood vessels had burst and was threatening at any moment to seep into his brain. He lay flat on his back, as he was to lie for the next six weeks. If he stayed absolutely still, and did not flood his system with more than a pint of fluid a day, he might live to know no more of his own youthful immortality save that he had nearly lost it.

Boyd did not know, as she shrugged her way along the beige gloss corridor, whether the patient she had come to see would still be alive in any accepted sense. She was pleased, as she rounded the corner, to see himself propped on pillows, looking round the room with a pocket mirror and tearing petals off a rose. He was framed in flowers, pale blue in colour, like the family eyes. His nose, like Boyd's was broken: tit for tat. His name, like hers, was Boyd.

'I never thought I'd see the day that my own grandmother outlived me.'

'You won't.'

'You mean I won't see it.'

There was a lot of death in the family that year. Intimations of, for those with health to hear them. The little sister had a car accident severing her foot; the grandmother bronchial pneumonia and an ulcer. For the women there was still time; their last breath would be enough.

'Anyway, it's a sad fact, but women live longer than men,' pronounced the grey figure in the metal bed, pain flashing over his face. Boyd's brother.

'Would you rather have been a woman?'

'Never. Not in a million years. No man would. I'd rather a man's death than life everlasting as a woman.'

Boyd smiled her relief. Time to zoom off again to

Candida. Tomorrow or tomorrow she would tell the women of the world the good news: lesbians had time to get it right, because lesbians live forever.

When these stories were written.

More Books From Onlywomen Press
Britain's only lesbian and radical feminist press

GOSSIP a new journal of lesbian feminist ethics   £2.50

Gossip: essential information; fast communication; opinions; theory; raw material for building our civilisation.
Ethics: responsible, liberating, creative standards to live by.
Featured in Issue One:
'The Mystery of Lesbians' by Julia Penelope – has the liberalisation of the women's liberation movement elbowed lesbians out?
'Lesbian Feminists and The Great Baby Con' by Sheila Shulman
'They don't know what to say to me' by Rosie Waite – disability and the lesbian community.

Subscriptions (3 issues) £6.50 UK;
£7.50 overseas surface / £10.50 air

WOMEN AGAINST VIOLENCE AGAINST WOMEN   £4.95
edited by dusty rhodes & Sandra McNeill

A collection of papers documenting three conferences held to discuss violence against women.
". . . the first radical step out of a huge sexual ghetto."

DIFFERENT ENCLOSURES poetry & prose of
Irena Klepfisz   £3.95

"I write as much out of a Jewish consciousness as I do out of a lesbian/feminist consciousness. They are both imbedded in my writing, for in many ways they are the same. Alienated. Threatened. Individual. Defiant."

THE WORK OF A COMMON WOMAN
by Judy Grahn   £2.95

including 'Edward They Dyke' and 'A Woman is Talking to Death'. Since the early 70s these poems have expressed and even initiated feminist activism.
". . . the most vivid and clearhoned series of portraits of women in any poetry I know." Adrienne Rich

Also by Anna Livia –
RELATIVELY NORMA   £2.95

Minnie flies to Australia to tell her mother she's a lesbian, and discovers, to her astonishment, that all the women in her family have their own lives to live, their own revelations to make. ". . . fast, furious and teeters agilely on the knife-edge of feminist farce."

THE NEEDLE ON FULL by Caroline Forbes   £3.95

Lesbian feminist science fiction
The charm of green furry extra-terrestrials; the satisfaction of eerie revenge against a rapist; the ethics of survival in a world devoid of, and devastated by, men; the intricacies of a relationship between two women locked together in the isolation of space.

ALTOGETHER ELSEWHERE by Anna Wilson   £2.95

Gripping epic of women as vigilantes, varied in age, race, class and sexuality; united only in desperation.
"A flickering, restless, adventurous novel – sometimes puzzling, often funny, always humming with energy – it flashes its lights down shadowy alleys all too often avoided."

CACTUS by Anna Wilson   £2.95

A lesbian classic
The story of Bea and Eleanor whose relationship broke up 20 years ago due to social pressure; of Ann and Dee who leave the city to concentrate on theirs.

THE REACH and other stories   £2.95
edited by Lilian Mohin & Sheila Shulman

The first collection of lesbian feminist short stories to come out of the British women's liberation movement. Humour, science fiction, fantasy and pathos in settings ranging from rural Scotland, the London Underground to a Greek island.